THE ELVEN STONES: ORPHAN

P A WILSON

Free ebook

Claim your copy of Obstacles of Magic when you use the QR code to sign up for my newsletter and learn more about Madeline's history with magic.

Chapter 1

The council members were long gone, but Willowvine felt their presence in the echoes of doubt that came in quiet moments. Every second they delayed in finding the Orphan Stone reinforced the fear it would be forgotten. That only she cared to place it back with its siblings. In her head, she knew it couldn't be true, but her heart was so used to feeling left behind she couldn't keep it hopeful.

The previous night, she'd been poring over records from Leafcreek's boxes of scrolls in the attic. The new Guardians would be clearing and organizing forever, she thought. Now, she stood at the window, looking across the sea toward the mainland. The last Stone of Power was there, she was sure.

"Willowvine," Springheart's voice broke into her reverie. "Come down for breakfast. It is time to talk."

She heard a weariness in his voice; it hadn't been there only weeks before. Was he tired of these quests?

She turned from the window and slipped into her shoes. If this turned out to be another session of speculation and delay, she would go for a run around the island afterward. Perhaps that would clear the gloom from her spirit.

The kitchen glowed with the early sunshine. Tom lifted the kettle from the stove; the boy had grown in the last few weeks. When they'd first met, he'd been shorter than she was, and his eagerness for adventure was evident in everything about him. She still saw the excitement in his eyes when he talked about their times on the road, but his recent experiences had darkened the joy. And now she had to look up a little to meet his eyes. Humans grew so fast.

Leafcreek sat wrapped in an intricately embroidered shawl despite the heat, which made her want to shuck her tunic for a light shirt. The old elf faded with every day that passed. Willowvine had never seen an elf die of old age, and this fading away didn't feel right. She renewed her vow to find the Orphan Stone before Leafcreek left them. He deserved to see his dream fulfilled before he closed his eyes forever. He wanted all three Stones returned to their rightful place in the center of the maze, and she would no longer delay the final mission.

"It is time to decide how this journey will commence," Springheart said. His long hair was tied back in a braid today, more formal than usual. Was he practicing for when they would rejoin Elven society? Or was she seeing things which didn't exist; perhaps he was as impatient as she to start the final leg of the journey.

"Finally," she said, accepting a plate from Tom and filling it. "We could leave tomorrow."

"And where are you headed?" Leafcreek asked. "Have your midnight studies revealed a clue?"

"It must be on the mainland," she said. "It's the only place big enough to hide something like that."

"Because we found the Stone of Abundance there?" Springheart asked. "We can't rush off on a hunch."

"The Stone of Family was there too," she said.

"Only because Maynard planned to sell it to the council," Springheart reminded her.

"Fine, we don't know where it is. We can't sit here forever either," she said, regretting the tone but not willing to apologize. She took a bite of a bread roll stuffed with butter and nuts to keep from speaking.

"This will not be a simple puzzle to find an object," Leafcreek said. "I think we need to bring a team together. One we have vetted, rather than one that rushed into being. I would like to avoid the situation we faced with Waterfeather. I am sorry to say, his cult has not been uprooted."

"It would be nice to make sure any companions are pleasant," Willowvine said. "Waterfeather being a saboteur was bad enough, but he didn't have to be such an ass."

They all chuckled at her joke. Maybe she could keep her eagerness to leave under control by entertaining everyone.

"It will not take too long," Leafcreek said. "I think a healer who will teach young Tom is a good idea. Perhaps someone who is also a scholar?"

"If I could learn more about my powers, maybe I could learn to be a healer for real," Tom said. "I would be happy to just heal animals but having the skill for people might save a life or two." He blushed and turned his attention to his tea.

"You are a healer. It means you have skill with all forms of life," Springheart said. "Having a seasoned one along would help you develop your talent. It is unfortunate that Callisra is not available."

"We will find another," Leafcreek said. "We also need to arrange for your supplies."

"Do not tire yourself," Lakewing said as she strode into the kitchen. Her years with the army were evident in the way she held herself at attention, and in the strong muscles of her arms and legs. The scar on her brow marked her as someone who had fought; not all the soldiers had. "Grasshorn and I will carry out your instruction, Master Leafcreek."

The new Guardians would be leaving on the next tide.

Willowvine was not sure they would have time to do anything Leafcreek needed for the quest. They had their own tasks.

"We will arrange for travel gear when we arrive in the City. We'll leave it with Zerenia, at her inn." Lakewing held up her hand to forestall any argument. "We will ask for recommendations for a healer at the Embassy, perhaps at others, not just the Elven one."

"That is more than I could expect," Leafcreek said. He put his tea mug on the table and picked up a berry. He examined it as he continued, "Now we have the job of finding the first steps."

"Grasshorn is delivering our baggage to the ship," Lakewing said. "He will return soon. Please think about what else we can do before we leave the City for our homes."

It felt like too little to say thank you, but that was all Willowvine could bring herself to do in the wake of Lakewing's kindness.

"Don't concern yourself," Lakewing said. "If I could come along, I would. I sometimes miss the excitement of a campaign. But I must make my arrangements to move here. I would be happy to find all three Stones of Power in place before I take on the role of Guardian with Grasshorn."

WILLOWVINE PACED BACK and forth while Tom and Springheart sat comfortably on the couch in front of the fire.

"The more we talk," she said. "The longer it takes for us to get started. I know we can't just run at it. But we can't be at a standstill either."

She leaned against the stone hearth, feeling the warmth soak into her back. The weather was changing, and soon travel would be too difficult, if not impossible.

"Complaining will not get us started." Springheart waved her to settle beside him. "It's not just the journey we must plan for. If your hopes come true, there will be a new future for us as well."

Willowvine looked over to Tom. As usual, he kept his thoughts to himself. She walked away from the fire and plopped onto the couch. Whining about not starting the quest didn't bring any satisfaction, but she didn't know what else to do. "Well, what are the things we absolutely need?"

"We already arranged that through Lakewing and Grasshorn," Springheart said. "They will leave soon, so she's right, it is a good time to think if we have forgotten anything."

"There is a lot we didn't ask for," Willowvine answered, trying to keep the frustration out of her voice. "If we knew everything we needed, we would be on the boat with them, or at least on the next one. Tom, what do you need in order for us to start?"

The boy squirmed in his seat. Willowvine had to remind herself that though he still looked like a young human, the last mission had forced him into an uncomfortable adulthood.

"If there is travel food and a bedroll, I don't need anything else. For the horses, we need feed and blankets. There's a few supplies I can pick up at the stable when we arrive on the mainland to deal with damaged hooves or scratches and scrapes."

Just like Tom to not think of anything beyond the practical needs. Willowvine decided she would spend some time teaching him to be a little more selfish as they rode. "We promised a teacher, and it is being arranged."

Springheart nudged her. "If we were to leave today, what direction would we go?"

She jumped up from the couch and started pacing again. "Exactly! We're doing nothing to find the clues we need."

"Master Leafcreek will find someone for us." Tom stood. "I'll make some tea. It's been a while since breakfast, and perhaps some snacks will help us think." He left the room before Willowvine could stop him.

"Leafcreek is so frail," she said. "Do you think he has the energy for this search?"

"We will provide him with what he needs," Springheart said. "I know you're impatient, but if we take a little time now, it may save days on the journey."

"I feel so useless," Willowvine admitted. "Every day that we wait for what we need feels like a year."

"When Leafcreek wakens, we will ask him how he intends to find us a scholar. I assume you don't wish to rush the process and end up with another Waterfeather." He patted the couch again. "Come sit down. All that pacing is not helping you manage your impatience. I'm sure we will be on our way in the next day or two."

Willowvine shrugged off her need to start the quest, shaking her hands to try to release the tension she could feel building. This time she sat more gracefully on the couch. Knowing Springheart was right didn't make it any easier to ignore the drive within her to finish their quest.

"When you have your freedom," Springheart said, "I mean, when your actions free all the orphans, what are your plans?"

"Not just my actions," she said. "I can't think of the future. I'm trying not to rely on the Council keeping their word. Or, perhaps only keeping their word in a strict sense, with no generosity of spirit."

"I understand, given our history with them, that you do not wish to get your hopes up. But this quest will be over whether they agree to accept orphans back into society or not. When we are no longer saving the world, what will we do?"

Willowvine massaged her temples, hoping it would distract her mind from trying to plan without any information. "I can't talk about it, Springheart."

He stood. "Then perhaps I will leave you to meditate."

Willowvine watched as he intercepted Tom at the doorway. She wasn't hungry, so missing the tea and snacks would not be a burden. But sitting here in this cozy space when she wished to go as quickly as she could to start her quest was not helping to clear her mind.

She crossed the room and took her cloak from the hook beside the front door. Some time alone walking the island might be the best for her.

THE WALK HAD DONE her good. The air was bracing rather than cold, and the constant wind reached in and pulled her doubts and fears away.

She opened the door to Leafcreek's cottage, realizing that soon she would begin to think of it as something other than that. She heard voices in the living room.

"We could linger in the City for a day or two," Grasshorn said.

"That is not necessary," Springheart said. "The sooner you are on your way, the sooner you will be back. If we need to, we can spend more time in the City plotting our own course."

Annoyed at Springheart's refusal of whatever they were offering, Willowvine tossed her cloak onto the hook and strode into the living room. Leafcreek was curled up on the couch that she had flounced on earlier. He was wrapped in a warm blanket, looking more frail than this morning. Lakewing and Grasshorn were standing by the fire, their travel bags at their feet.

"I'm glad I didn't miss you," Willowvine said. "What was this offer I heard you making?" If she could override Springheart's words, Willowvine would have them spend as much time as possible in the City.

"We suggested doing a little research in the embassy library.

It might save you valuable time." Lakewing stepped away from the hearth. "We could leave any information we found with Zerenia."

Willowvine was about to agree when Springheart caught her gaze. From his position by the window he glanced briefly at Leafcreek and then back at her. She felt a flush of shame flood her cheeks. If the new Guardians were not back soon, the Stones of Power might be left without a protector.

"Thank you for the offer," she said. "It is probably better we do our own research. Without knowing what to ask, I think doing the work itself may shed light on the knowledge we seek."

"Do not fear that I shall die any moment." Leafcreek gave a dry chuckle. "But there is wisdom in Willowvine's words. And I would guess any notes you leave would not satisfy their curiosity. That the work, rather than speeding their quest, would only delay yours."

Willowvine's cheeks burned hotter. Now it felt like he was saying she didn't trust the two new Guardians, which was far from the truth.

Lakewing laughed and picked up her baggage. "Then we will go. We will send a bird with confirmation of what we left with Zerenia. I hope you're able to depart soon; it must be difficult to wait for this last quest to start. I look forward to seeing you at the ceremony to replace the Stone of Orphan."

When they were alone, Willowvine glanced around, realizing she had not seen Tom.

"The boy is at the stable," Leafcreek said. "He has gained a reputation. There was an accident, and the horse needed his attention. The stableman sent for him without any reservations about his lack of years."

Willowvine wondered how much in demand Tom would be after receiving training from someone skilled in healing all manner of creatures. "It's likely best that he is not here while we do our research. It must be boring to watch us scry."

"Yes. For him it would just be watching us bent over a bowl of water." Springheart stoked the fire before turning back to Leafcreek. "If you're feeling strong enough, I suggest we have a little food and then begin our search."

Willowvine was relieved that someone else took on the role of nagging to get started. She offered to set up lunch and left the room.

Chapter 2

She filled the scrying bowl with clear water from the spring near Leafcreek's home. This felt like they were taking the first step on the quest for the Orphan Stone. The frustrations of the morning still niggled in the back of her mind, but she knew she could quiet them enough to help Leafcreek reach his friend.

She carried the bowl into the warm living room. Leafcreek, sitting on the floor supported by cushions and warmed by the fire, beckoned her.

"Springheart will be back soon," he said. "Let us see if we can center your thoughts. I would like it if you could contact Treepond."

"She is your friend," Willowvine said as she placed the bowl in front of Leafcreek. "She is an important person, too important to answer my call."

Leafcreek smiled. "You will find that is not true." He reached across the bowl for her hands. "You may need her help along the journey. I also think you need to become closer to other elves."

It's not my choice. "They tend to avoid me."

"Perhaps, but Treepond is different." He must have seen the reluctance on her face because he added, "If you wish to join Elven society, you cannot expect others to take the first steps."

There was no point in arguing. Willowvine sighed and nodded for Leafcreek to start the meditation.

"We will go into your past," he said gently, "to a time when you were happy."

Willowvine searched her memories. She was orphaned so young that it was hard to find a memory of her parents. Then she recalled how her gang had taken her in. At the beginning, before they made her use her power for stealing. Sitting at the campfire in the evenings, telling stories, laughing, it was the first time she felt loved and safe.

"I have one," she whispered.

"Imagine across this memory a veil of worries and anger."

The fact she had to search so hard for a memory increased her anger, making this a much easier task. The veil she saw in her mind became gray, thick, and woven from coarse thread.

"Now, you must try to remove the veil."

Willowvine tried to picture a large hand lifting the veil, but it was too heavy. She tried imagining rain washing it away as though it were a layer of ash, but it wouldn't move.

"I can't," she said.

"You must," Leafcreek said. "The veil will smother all your hopes."

Tears of frustration pressed on her eyes. In her mind she saw a wind blow across the material, ruffling the edges but not budging it.

"The power is there for you, if you trust it," Leafcreek said.

She let the wind die down and concentrated on real things, not her emotions; Leafcreek's hand, the soft carpet beneath her, the warmth on her face from the fire. Taking a deep breath, she let go of Leafcreek's hands and reached for the veil as though it were real. In her mind her hands came down and plucked at the material, lifting it away from the happy memory underneath.

"Now you will be ready when we scry," Leafcreek said.

Willowvine wondered how he knew that she'd succeeded but kept the thought to herself. The veil would not be gone forever, but perhaps the next time she performed this meditation, the memories would be easier to find, and the veil would be lighter.

Springheart joined them as she let her mind return to the task. He placed a twig in the bowl, along with a drop of rosemary oil.

"That should help us with the spell," he said. "Oak for strength and rosemary for clarity."

Afraid the peace of the meditation would fade, Willowvine began the spell. She reached out to join hands, and then bent over the bowl and breathed Treepond's name onto the surface.

The elf's image appeared after only a few seconds. Like all her kind, it was hard to determine her exact age. Definitely not young, but still with many years to live. Her white hair was braided back into an intricate knot. She stared into Willowvine's eyes. "It is good to see you," she said.

"You remember me?" Willowvine asked.

"How could I forget someone so vital to the world?" She glanced over her shoulder as though someone had interrupted with a question. Then she turned back. "You are preparing for the next mission?"

"As fast as we can," Willowvine said. "It's not fast enough, really."

Treepond laughed. "I can understand that. What do you need of me?"

Willowvine turned to Leafcreek for help.

He leaned forward. "Are you able to talk freely?"

"No one will hear us," Treepond said. "A trusted ally guards my door."

"Have you learned more of this secret society?" Leafcreek asked.

"It will take patience," Treepond said. "I cannot ask openly."

"Would it take less time if you were asking for someone other than orphans?" Willowvine regretted the words as soon as they slipped out.

Treepond lowered her gaze. "I see how you might feel that way, Willowvine. Let me assure you, I am sympathetic to your desire. This prejudice damages us all."

"I'm sorry," Willowvine said. "My impatience is defeating my courtesy."

"Never apologize for your passion," Treepond said. "Perhaps there is something else I can do to help you."

Willowvine didn't know what to ask for. They had so many needs, and all of them important in her mind.

"Do you think you could find us someone to train our healer?" Springheart asked. "We owe Tom a great debt, and it would relieve some of our fears if a companion came with a recommendation."

"Thank you for your trust." Treepond closed her eyes and gave a small nod. "No one comes to mind, but it should be a simple matter. Do you have any preferences for talent?"

Willowvine let Springheart continue with the conversation. She should have thought of Tom's needs.

"Someone who can travel with us," Springheart said. "And someone with patience. Tom is barely more than a child, and his confidence is fragile."

"I will leave word with Zerenia Alewife. If there is nothing else, I fear we are tiring Leafcreek."

Willowvine thanked Treepond and closed the connection. It was fortunate that they had made friends with Zerenia. The only other place in the City where they could reasonably leave messages for each other was the embassy, and the less Willowvine had to do with the Elven officials the better.

She glanced over to see Leafcreek dozing. He would be restoring his energy for a few hours. The day was more than half over, and her desire to leave the island grew stronger than ever.

There were only so many times that she could go out for a walk to burn off her energy. While Leafcreek rested and Springheart met with Tom, it left Willowvine with no one to talk to. The only place she had not explored in the house was the library. Leafcreek claimed the right to do that research. But now she couldn't leave it undone. Surely in the library of the Guardian of the Stones she would find information on the Stones of Power.

The entrance to the room was tucked under the stairs. A small door even for an elf. Willowvine bent to enter, leaving it open. There was no light source she could see, and she wasn't willing to wait for Leafcreek to activate any spells. What light drifted in from the hallway illuminated the room sufficiently to see that this was not a traditional library. While she may not be able to read the titles in the gloom, she could see stacks of books in random piles leaning against the base of a bookshelf, some left open with pages overlapping; a sight that would have made even the least experienced keeper weep.

She knew there must be a spell in place; one which convinced spiders and vermin to set their webs and nests else-where. The low roof and dark corners seemed free of evidence of the first, and the air smelled of books, not of vermin.

She headed for the small table set at the center of the room, thinking the open books were evidence Leafcreek had been searching for information. What else would he be looking for now other than clues to the Orphan Stone?

She carefully lifted the books to read the spines. A

genealogy of the Guardians of the Stones all the way back to the first one. Not only did it contain a detailed and ornate family tree, but each Guardian had used the book as a journal of sorts. At a quick glance, Willowvine saw entries regarding the best plants to use with the spells to hide the maze from the sight of others and a long list of incantations to be spoken in the individual rites. Nothing even mentioning the Orphan Stone, or any of them individually.

The other open book revealed itself to be a catalog of all the books in the library. A few scattered parchments contained copies of titles with lines drawn through them. Leafcreek had been searching his library. Willowvine realized she was not the only person frustrated by the wait. It must have galled Leafcreek to be working so hard and not finding anything.

"Do you need light?" Leafcreek asked from the door, his voice barely above a whisper.

Willowvine nodded. Before she could say that she would cast the spell if Leafcreek told her the words, he waved his hand and muttered a phrase. Dots of light woke in the corners of the room, brightening steadily until Leafcreek waved his hand again. He joined her, taking the one seat at the table.

"If we only had all the time in the world to do the research," Leafcreek said. "I tire too easily to study the contents of my small library for more than an hour. I always intended to organize it, but a book or scroll would take my attention and hours would pass before I looked away."

Willowvine knew they could delay leaving if it meant they would find valuable information, but she felt the urgency of this final quest too strongly to spend much time in this stuffy closet. "Perhaps you will find something while we travel. A bird would find us with a message."

"Do not fret, Willowvine. It is not my intention to hold you here longer than needed. I made arrangements for you to travel on the first tide tomorrow."

Willowvine glanced up from the page of the book she was reading. "Did Treepond respond? You should have called me. I could have taken that burden from you."

Leafcreek smiled and patted her arm. "No news came. I decided I must bow to your wishes. There is no point in waiting for help which might not come. Grasshorn and Lakewing will be back and I will spend my time looking through this." He waved his hand around the crowded walls.

"Would the seeker spell work here?" Willowvine asked. The seeker spell was used in libraries to locate information. Singing it would cause a book with any information requested to glow.

"I never thought I would be in this position, so I did not create one. It is best, I think, to look through this catalog for inspiration."

"Then I will do it. Everything I need for the journey is packed. I can search in here until it is time to leave."

"Child, you need rest and food. But perhaps a few hours of searching would be of value."

"Is there a record of the time when all the Stones were in place?" Willowvine asked. The list of publications in the catalog was dauntingly long and not indexed.

Leafcreek rose and took a bundle of scroll sheets from a dark shelf. "It will say nothing about their disappearance, but this is my great grandfather's journal.

Willowvine placed the sheets on the table and made sure that Leafcreek sat before opening them. "This starts on the day he became Guardian. Would your father have a similar journal?"

"It is here somewhere," Leafcreek said. "It will be my first goal. Again, whatever we find will not describe the disappearance; whoever the Guardian was at the time would have died defending the Stones and I have no recollection of such a thing. But perhaps there will be clues to another book, and then another."

Willowvine unrolled the first few sheets. "Look," she said, pointing at a drawing. "He shows the maze with only two Stones. But the space for the Orphan Stone is not as overgrown as it is now." She gazed around her again, hoping for inspiration. "Is your great-great-grandfather's journal here?"

"I checked in there; it mentions nothing of the Stone being taken."

"But it was there in his time?"

Leafcreek rose from the chair, more slowly than a moment ago, and bent to a pile of scrolls near the door. Willowvine swallowed the grief that flooded her heart at the reminder that the old elf was close to the end of his life.

"Here," he said, wheezing and tossing the scroll to her.

"Is there a drawing?"

He sat and then held out his hand. "Yes. If my memory is not truly gone. Let me look."

It felt like he was going to unroll and read every sheet before speaking. Willowvine itched to take the scroll from him, but Leafcreek nodded and pointed to a sketch before she reached her limit.

"He was not as good an artist as my great-grandfather."

The maze was clearly if lifelessly drawn. In the center, three Stones nestled together as though they were one. Willowvine recognized the Family and Abundance Stones. Her eyes were drawn tightly to the third one. Roughly triangular, almost like the keystone in an arch, it was a little larger that than the other two.

"What is this?" She pointed to a mark at the edge of the drawing.

Leafcreek leaned over her shoulder. "Hmm. It looks very like the sign for the Library at the Well. Perhaps they verified the sketch? I never noticed it before."

If someone didn't look closely, the mark could be mistaken for a clump of grass. But it was not.

"Then I suppose we will find ourselves there again," Willowvine said. Knowing the Well was sealed, and the creature gone, didn't stop the fear that shivered her blood at the memory of that battle.

"It is a long way from here. I hope you will find information well before that," Leafcreek said.

Chapter 3

Knowing their mission was vital to Willowvine and Springheart, to the elves as a whole, didn't stop Leafcreek regretting that they had to leave. He doubted his life would continue long enough to see the final Stone placed, and that meant this day was his last opportunity to be with people he had come to think of as family. In fact, they were more like family than his biological child. They would both have made good Guardians if their paths leaned that way. But their destiny was to wander, to make things right, to bring light to the darkness.

"Enough dwelling on loss," he said, pushing himself up from the couch. There were things he could continue to do. It was not yet time for that last aching moment of farewell.

He would walk the maze of the Stones daily as long as he had the energy. Leafcreek took a warm cloak from the hanger by the back door. This passage along the maze would be slow. He would contemplate his coming death. A fitting thing in this world.

He paused at the first stone, stepping on it and reaching for a fond memory. His father leading him through the first of the rites. It had always baffled him that the Stones of Power were not visible until he reached the inner circle of the path. The maze was small, only three rings. The ground was flat, and yet, there was a muddying at the center. A good protection, or at least it had been until the Scree had stolen one.

He drew up a new memory with each step. Reliving happy times in his life. Another day, he would reflect on his mistakes.

As he entered the final circle, Leafcreek glanced to the center. The carefully crafted layer of peace fled as if a gale had dissolved a mist. The two Stones still lay there, but they had moved.

Less than an inch, but the Stones had nestled together as if they were pieces of a puzzle only yesterday; the space for the Orphan Stone clear. Now the gap was wider; clearly the threat to Cartref was not removed by the return of the Stone of Abundance.

Their mission was no longer simply a way for him to die in peace and Willowvine to achieve acceptance; it was vital to the health of the world.

WILLOWVINE FILLED the last clear space on the paper with notes. She didn't know if there was value to the information she found in Leafcreek's books, but the small task lessened the feeling of being shackled. It was an hour to the next sailing and another opportunity to start the quest would be lost. Another day.

Until she was aboard, she couldn't quite believe they would leave in the morning. There was always one more reason to delay a little longer.

The back door opened, and the slight breeze of fresh air drew her attention away from the next book.

"Willowvine? Springheart?" Leafcreek's voice carried urgency.

She pushed away from the table and hurried to the kitchen. "Springheart is still out with Tom," she said. Then, seeing the fear on the old elf's face, she rushed to his side. "What has happened?" *Please do not die yet.*

"When will they return?"

"Soon," Willowvine said. Taking Leafcreek's hand, she tried to rub some warmth into the cold skin.

"You must leave now, on this tide," he said. "Your things are ready?"

Her heart leapt. It was like she'd wished this into being. If only she could be sure that Leafcreek would survive. "Yes, we can go at a moment's notice," she said. "Let me get you some tea."

"Only until Tom and Springheart return. You must leave as soon as they join us."

"What happened?" She filled the kettle and wondered if she should seek out Springheart rather than wait.

"The Stones are moving again."

The kettle banged on the stove as she suddenly had no strength to hold it. "I'll go find them."

"No, you must bring all of your belongings together so there will be no delay."

"The bags are packed, Leafcreek," she said. "We were leaving tomorrow anyway. Don't fret so much, it will weaken you."

He waved away her concern. "I will sleep and restore myself when I am alone. That and trying to protect the Stones is all I have left to do when you leave."

"You have much more to do," she said. "You will help us return the Orphan Stone to its place. You cannot die until we succeed."

Leafcreek stopped fussing and smiled at her. "I will do my best."

The kettle boiled, and she poured water in the pot to steep

the healing herbs. Just as she finished, the front door opened and Tom ran into the kitchen.

"We sent birds to the mainland," he said, then something on her face must have alerted him. "Something changed."

Springheart joined them before Leafcreek could answer.

"Tom, can you try some healing?" Springheart said as he dropped to sit beside Leafcreek's chair. "You are almost transparent with wear. Let the boy give you some energy."

Willowvine wanted to drag both of them out of the room and down to the docks. The ships would be leaving in less than an hour. They still needed to negotiate fares.

Tom made him drink half the tea before laying his hands on Leafcreek's chest. Willowvine watched, but there was no sign of the energy transferring. Then a little color shaded Leafcreek's cheeks.

"I'll get our gear," she said, leaving the room while Leafcreek explained.

When she had the bags in the front hall, she pulled their cloaks off the hook and returned to the kitchen. "Let's go."

"One moment more, please." Leafcreek reached for a key. "Tom, go to my room and open the locked drawer in my desk. Bring what you find there."

"The transfer boats will be leaving soon," Willowvine said.

"You will need money and letters of introduction when you arrive on the mainland. It is not like before. You are, perhaps, not welcome, but allowed to travel the lands. I have arranged for help if you should need it. The letters are important."

Willowvine doubted that the new permissions for orphans would be widely accepted, but Leafcreek wouldn't delay them unless he thought he was helping.

Tom returned with a heavy pouch and a handful of sealed scrolls. He passed them to Leafcreek.

"The pouch is full of coin. Please, do not hesitate to use the money. I will have no need of it."

Willowvine wanted to say that he should keep the money, but she knew he spoke the truth. The dead needed no coin. She took the pouch and tucked it into her tunic.

"The letters are labeled," Leafcreek said. "These are friends. While they are not the kind of scholars to help you find the Stone, they will protect and shelter you if you are in need."

"Thank you," Springheart said. "I'm sure that these will be as valuable as the coin."

"Yes," Willowvine said. "You have always helped us and now we can fulfill your dream."

Leafcreek chuckled. "Yes, my dream and yours. But only if I allow you to leave. Do not fret too much. The captain has been warned that he might need to accept extra passengers. You may not be comfortable, but you will find passage."

Willowvine bent and kissed Leafcreek's forehead. "Don't wear yourself out while we're gone."

"Grasshorn and Lakewing will ensure I am still here when you return. Just do not take too long." Leafcreek smiled and then said his goodbyes.

Willowvine handed Springheart and Tom their cloaks and dragged them from the kitchen.

Chapter 4

A day later, the shuttle boat pilot had barely finished tying up when Willowvine sprang from the seat to the ladder. She scrambled to the top and dragged herself over the edge to the unmoving land.

Tom knelt beside where she lay on the cobbles. "Let me heal you."

"Save your energy," she said. "The only cure for seasickness is land."

"If I knew you would get sick, I might have done something."

Willowvine rolled to her side. The reliability of land to stay firm and still calmed whatever part of her rebelled when she ventured onto the sea. "It doesn't happen every time," she said.

The other passengers climbed up and then strode past her with no acknowledgment.

"I know. It was fine when we went to the island. When we come back, I could..." he laughed. "How about I promise to learn a cure?"

"I think we will all benefit from anything you can do to alleviate her distress," Springheart said.

He passed Tom his pack and slung his own over his shoulder. He looked at Willowvine with a question on his face.

She stood, and nothing tilted. "Let's go. Maybe Zerenia will have some good news." She took her pack and marched across the wharf.

Zerenia's inn was only a short walk from the docks, but far enough to give Willowvine a chance to observe the City. It hustled more than the last time she'd passed through. More people rushing to and from the stores and warehouses lining the wharf. More people calling out their wares from the side of their stalls. Just more people, in more variety, than had been there a week ago when they carried the Stone of Abundance to the ship.

It was such a short time, but in the process of reaching the street, Willowvine had seen three Elven women with the dark lines of pregnancy on their faces. Three in only a moment when she'd only seen one in her life before. She hoped the recent movement of the Stones would not bode evil for these children.

"Excuse my impertinence, but are you Willowvine?" A fourth pregnant elf stood before her.

For a moment, Willowvine considered lying. After the horror of the passage, she wasn't sure she had the patience for politeness. But she couldn't bring herself to do that to someone carrying new life into the world. "I am."

"Thank you," the woman said. "The bards are telling tales of your fight to restore the Stone of Abundance."

Willowvine's throat tightened and her eyes held tears on the edge of falling. Simon had not been idle. She cleared her throat, afraid she would cry if she didn't push the emotions down. "I wish only good fortune for your child."

"My name is Elderroot. If you ever need help, look for my family. We are not influential, but we are willing."

The elf ran toward the shadows of a side street without

waiting for a response. Willowvine wasn't sure what she would have said anyway.

"Now you choose to dawdle," Springheart said as he stepped up to join her.

"Did you hear what she said?"

"Yes. Perhaps we are no longer so reviled. But we should get to Zerenia's."

"Cartref works fast," Tom said. "How long until the babies are born?"

Willowvine didn't share her worry that these babies would only be safe when they breathed their own air. If they failed to return the Stone of Orphan, or if that didn't satisfy Cartref, perhaps the children would never be born. "Like humans, I think. About nine months."

Willowvine followed Tom and Springheart down the narrow street leading to Zerenia's inn. The light changed from shadow to white brightness between buildings. The encounter bewildered her. To think some elves thought she was valuable fragmented her understanding of the world.

The sight of the inn sign broke into her thoughts. She rubbed her face. It wasn't the time to think about her beliefs, but perhaps it was time to acknowledge they were prejudices; she would give that more thought when the Stone was replaced.

"How long will we be here?" Tom asked.

"It depends," Springheart answered. "At least a few hours while we gather what we need. Why?"

"I've never spent a lot of time with a Mariai before." He blushed and looked at the ground. "I heard they are able to do things to change your future."

Willowvine stepped up next to Tom. "Some have the gift. They aren't bad people, just able to read prophecy. They don't do anything to change it, except maybe to give you a choice."

Springheart slipped into the inn while Willowvine tried to

make Tom comfortable enough to go in. If he carried this feeling inside, Zerenia might sense it. She was usually reasonable but could be sensitive. If she took any kind of offense, Zerenia would retreat to her visions and that might mean days before she would emerge.

"Like knowing your future means you can do things differently?" Tom straightened, putting on a brave face if Willowvine read him correctly.

"Yes," she said. "Do you want to know your future?"

"You said not all Mariai can do it, right?"

She couldn't let him go inside assuming Zerenia was not a seer. "That's right, but our host is one of the best."

"I don't want to know." Tom's eyes were wide. He was trying to look unconcerned, but Willowvine heard the fear in his voice.

"Then don't ask," she said. "Zerenia won't blurt out anything. You're safe unless you ask her and pay her."

He stared into her eyes long enough for Willowvine to start thinking of errands to send him on so he wouldn't have to enter the inn.

"Okay. I guess we should go in." He didn't wait for her to lead, just marched into the dim interior.

Willowvine pushed down a smile. Tom, for all his skill and common wisdom, was still a child.

Inside, Springheart was speaking to Zerenia. The woman was only about five and a half feet tall, but she looked down at him. Her gray hair was pulled up in a topknot as usual, leaving her facial scars visible. Willowvine realized how fierce Zerenia must look to Tom, so she asked him to watch the bags while she joined the conversation.

"I know a healer who has a taste for adventure," Zerenia said. "He will join us this evening. Will it be acceptable for all three of you to share one room?" She glanced over at Tom.

"That will be fine, and I thank you for your hospitality," Willowvine said. "We won't be here long."

"Zerenia has offered a vision," Springheart said. Then, turning to their host, he added, "We'll send Tom to the room while we wait for your words."

"No, he needs to hear the vision," Zerenia said. "You know this, Springheart. Each person will interpret the vision from a different perspective. You will not be sure which view is of use without all."

"I'll talk to him," Willowvine said. "He's nervous, Zerenia. I'll need some time. When will you be ready to enter the trance? Will it make a difference? I just promised him this very thing wouldn't happen."

"An hour. That will give you time to settle and clean up." Zerenia left them and entered her chambers.

"Why clean up?" Willowvine asked. "Do I smell?"

"You've been sick for the whole trip."

"Fine. I'll wash after talking to Tom."

Springheart put his hand on her shoulder. "Go take care of yourself. I will talk to the boy."

"But I told him he wouldn't have to..."

"I know, and it means I should tell him things have changed."

Not sure whether she felt relief or guilt, Willowvine nodded and then followed the maid who led her down a dark hall.

FEELING MORE civilized after a quick bath, Willowvine picked through the pile of clothes in her pack; a clean body needed clean garments. There was nothing that could be described as dressy, but her travel clothes were new, and new was the best she could do right now. Tom and Springheart were cleaning up, giving her the privacy to change. Whatever Springheart had said to make Tom come to the session had worked. The boy didn't seem to carry any grudge about the change. He might be too forgiving for his own good.

"Are you ready?" Springheart called from the hall.

Willowvine pulled her tunic over her head, straightened her trousers and ran to follow them to Zerenia's chambers.

When they settled, Willowvine flanked by Springheart and Tom, Zerenia doused all but one candle.

"I will enter a trance," she said. "I may be there for a long time. Please do not worry for me. I will be safe. You must heed what I say while I am in the world of prophecy. I do not always speak, but I will also not recall anything I say."

Tom shifted on his cushion. Willowvine glanced at him, saw he wanted to ask a question, and gave him a nod.

"You said it might be a long time. How will we know you are safe? If it is days, do we feed you?"

Zerenia smiled. "You think of the health of others even through your fear. You will be a great healer. I do not need a prophecy to be sure of that." She placed a bowl of incense beside the candle. "My servants will take care of me if I am there that long. I do not believe I will be. This time I am called to the world and I go to take what is offered. It is when I enter asking for wisdom that it takes longer to find an answer."

Zerenia lit the incense and breathed in the smoke. "Refreshments will be brought. Please, eat and drink as much as you need. Don't speak until I return."

Willowvine watched as Zerenia's eyes closed and a gentle smile grew on her lips. Then she was gone. Her body still sat across from them, but her spirit was elsewhere.

An hour later, Willowvine wondered if they were allowed to move. Her back was stiffening, and she felt an itch between her shoulder blades. The door opened without a sound, and a servant placed a tray of refreshments on the floor. After the seasickness, Willowvine was surprised at her hunger. She reached for a plate of fruit and silently offered to pour tea. Her companions declined.

As she placed the first slice of melon in her mouth, Zerenia's eyes popped open. "Trust not the fair and helpful." Her eyes closed again.

By the time Willowvine swallowed the fruit, Zerenia was breathing deeply. The seer straightened and then opened her eyes again.

"There is danger and destruction where the item you seek sits," she said. "I could not see it. I heard screams that echoed from the ancient past. I smelled blood and fire."

"Will there be a battle?" Springheart asked.

"I could not tell if the battle was now, in the past, or in the future," Zerenia said as she poured tea. "I know that where you seek is soaked, or will be, in death."

"Is there more?" Tom asked.

"That is all I was able to find." She sipped and took a fig from the plate.

"You spoke while you were in the other place," Willowvine said. "Perhaps that will help you interpret what you saw?"

Zerenia shrugged.

"You said, 'trust not the fair and helpful.' It should mean something to you." Tom leaned forward. "Does it?"

"It may, if I give it thought," Zerenia said. "But you do not have time to wait for my pondering."

Springheart stood. "I know this drains you, Zerenia. We will leave you to rest."

Willowvine had more questions, but she knew they would go unanswered. Zerenia was a simple messenger and left the interpretation to the customer.

Chapter 5

Tom sat at the dinner table and watched the people around him. So many types of people gathered together that he couldn't help but stare like a farm boy. The most interesting, and frightening, were the three Scree sitting at a table in the corner. He'd never seen a Scree up close, as none of them visited Lady Madeline or Sir Jode. He figured ending a blood feud stopped the killing but left resentment.

The Scree stayed quiet, but Tom knew that could change and he needed to be ready to run.

"They won't attack in here," Willowvine said. "They might not attack at all. Things have changed, Tom. We should try to learn from history, not let it burden us."

He turned to look at Willowvine. He knew the legend. She'd received help from a Scree when they closed the Well at the Center of the World. "They still look fierce. If the Scree are ready to be peaceful, why do they still weave bones into their braids?"

Willowvine laughed. "Try to think of it as a fashion statement."

"They are old bones," Springheart said. "I don't think a Scree has killed since Madeline sealed the well."

Tom turned back to look at them. Maybe Willowvine had it right, but he would hold back on forgiving. Not so long ago, one of their kind had tried to destroy the Summer Lands.

But only he seemed worried. Between the goblins in the corner, the humans at the next table, and the Sylphs near the door, it may as well have been a family dinner for all the care anyone had.

"Good evening." An elf stood beside their table.

Tom hadn't noticed his approach. That would be a problem on the road. How had he become so unaware of their surroundings in such a short time?

The newcomer was different from Springheart and Willowvine. They were typical elves, short, pointy eared, blue eyes and white hair. This elf had the same ears and stood shorter than Springheart. His eyes were deep green and his hair black.

"And to you," Willowvine said. "Can we assist you?"

The elf laughed. "I have forgotten my manners. I am Dawnriver. You are expecting me, I think."

"We are expecting someone," Tom said. He wasn't going to give this Dawnriver any information; he fit Zerenia's warning too well.

"You must be Tom." Dawnriver approached and held out his hand to shake.

Tom stared at the hand but didn't take it.

"I am to teach you healing. And to join you on your adventure." The last was said to the whole party.

Tom stood and shook Dawnriver's hand, keeping his grip firm. "We don't want the entire world to hear about our plans."

"Take a seat, Dawnriver," Willowvine said. She gave Tom a glare.

He smiled back. He knew what she wanted, but that would wait for later. Everything that had happened since he agreed to leave home and ride with Willowvine taught him not to accept help at face value. Didn't Willowvine remember Zerenia's words?

"Are you prepared to travel?" Springheart asked.

Tom was happy not to join the conversation. If he could observe Dawnriver, maybe he would be able to explain the gut feeling he had that something was wrong.

"I am. My bags are in the lobby. Our hostess told me we would be departing immediately."

"Before dawn," Willowvine said. "You can put your things in our room. There's plenty of floor space if you need a place for the night."

"Can you tell us something of your background?" Springheart asked.

Good! At least someone was asking questions and not just blindly welcoming this stranger.

"I see Zerenia has been her usual stingy self with information," Dawnriver said. He tested the teapot. "This is cold. Let's get a fresh pot."

"Do you need food?" Willowvine asked as she turned to summon the maid.

"A meal would be much appreciated," Dawnriver said. "The life of a wandering healer is often lonely and hungry."

"You were going to tell us about your qualifications," Tom said.

"Yes. The short of it is that I trained at the academy as a healer. My future plans had been to join the army, but since we are at peace, the army is diminished. I chose to roam the world, seeking my future." Dawnriver smiled at the maid when she placed a platter of food on the table. "My family and I do not agree on how the world works. I thought I would be happier away from them, at least for a while."

"How do you know Zerenia?" Tom wished the Mariai woman was here to vouch for Dawnriver, but she'd closed her door after the vision.

He'd tried to talk to her an hour or so later, filled with questions about the world she visited, full of surprise that the experience made him more curious than afraid. The maid refused to let him knock on the door, adamant Zerenia needed rest and would not emerge until after they had departed.

"A long time ago, she knew my mother," Dawnriver said. His face lost its smile when he spoke. Then, as if he realized he showed some emotion, he grinned and added, "Part of the reason my family and I don't agree."

"Perhaps we should retire," Springheart said. "Dawnriver, please join us when you have eaten."

Dawnriver stared into Tom's eyes. "Then I passed the test?"

"I need training. And I expect Zerenia chose the right person." Tom couldn't bring himself to fully welcome Dawnriver to their team.

WILLOWVINE STARED at the bags piled in the corner of the room. Waiting to start their journey was worse now than the last few days on the island. The final few supplies were vital to their trip and wouldn't arrive at the stable until early tomorrow morning. Their road passed a few villages, but it was likely the supplies they needed wouldn't be available. So, the soonest they could start on the journey was dawn.

She crept from their room so she wouldn't disturb the others; they slept as if tomorrow wasn't the most important day in her life. She wouldn't risk walking the streets this late in the day, but a pot of tea in the dining area might settle her nerves enough to let her rest.

She sat at a table on the edge of the room, giving her a

view of the inn from front to back. She was not alone; the Scree merchants still haggled, their voices louder now with the aid of several bottles of wine. Willowvine wondered how they kept track of the negotiations when they were clearly drunk.

A flicker of movement in the lobby caught her eye. Zerenia was out of her room. Willowvine stood, hoping to talk to the seer; to try for more clarity, or more information. Another elf approached Zerenia before Willowvine could take more than a step. She couldn't hear any details, but their actions appeared friendly. After a moment, Zerenia nodded toward the dining area and then retreated to her room. Willowvine cursed the loss of her opportunity and returned to her seat.

The elf came toward Willowvine and she saw that it was a girl, probably not much older than herself. Her hair, drawn back in a leather thong, showed the multiple jewels attached to both ears. Her eyes sparkled blue with her generous smile as she stopped beside Willowvine's table.

"I think you might be waiting for me," the girl said.

Willowvine poured tea into her cup. "Why do you think that?" She had enough strangers to manage already.

"Zerenia. She said you would have need of my skills." The girl sat. "Did she forget to tell you I was available?"

Willowvine suspected that Zerenia forgot nothing. If she hadn't witnessed their exchange a few moments ago, she would have sent the girl packing.

"What skills?" She wouldn't turn away help without knowing if she needed it.

"You are in search of something," the girl said.

"How did you know that?"

"My contact wishes to stay in the shadows."

Treepond? Leafcreek? One of the Guardians? No, they had no need for secrecy.

"Isn't it considered polite to introduce yourself?" Willowvine asked. Perhaps the girl's name would be familiar.

"Of course, how could I forget. My name is Cornflower, and you are the famous Willowvine."

There had been a girl with the same name in her old gang. Not the same person, Willowvine knew, and not an uncommon name.

"Not famous," Willowvine said. "What is your skill?"

Before the girl could answer, Dawnriver joined them at the table. "Tea? What a good idea." He waved to the server and indicated he wanted another pot and two more cups. "Who is your friend?"

Cornflower smiled at him in a way that conveyed more than pleasure at meeting someone. Willowvine wondered what in her past had made her behave that way.

"I came to see if I could be of help to your mission," Cornflower said. "I hear you need someone to research obscure histories."

"How did you come to hear that?" Dawnriver asked with an edge to his voice.

Willowvine sipped her tea and watched them. It was much easier to assess that way. If either of them posed a danger to the recovery of the Stone, she believed it would come to her if she simply observed.

"I know your mission is not public," Cornflower said. "The person who told me said to be discreet. I think she meant me to keep her identity a secret from people I don't know."

"It will be difficult for you to find allies if you are unable to be honest," Dawnriver said.

"Our lives are not meant to be easy," Cornflower said.

The subtext of the conversation remained beyond Willowvine. It was time to drag them back to the real world. The fresh tea arrived in time for her to use it as an interruption.

She poured and said, "We still have not heard what value you will bring to us."

Cornflower's smile dimmed a little at the question. Then she regained her sunny appearance. "I am skilled in finding the truth in riddles and uncovering clues in obscure documents. I make my living gleaning details that people find valuable."

Willowvine suspected that the value of Cornflower's discoveries might be in them staying hidden rather than being made public. She sipped her tea to stall for time. The skill would help, there was no doubt in her mind. But adding another stranger to their party was risky.

"I think we have everyone we need to complete our task," Dawnriver said.

Willowvine placed her cup on the table and stood. "Such skills might be useful. Meet us at the stable at dawn." She left them and headed back to the room.

Chapter 6

Springheart tightened the strap as he saddled Blaze, the horse Tom assigned to him. Willowvine had done her share of currying the animals to prepare them for the journey, but her excitement bled out and infected the horses with a jittery eagerness to go. It would be useful when they traveled, as eager horses have more stamina, but for now it just made everything harder.

He watched as Willowvine sorted through the various supplies, making sure the loads were balanced and there was nothing missing at the last moment. He stood close enough to hear her mumbling as she inventoried their belongings. It was busy work; they had sufficient supplies, and they could replenish along the way if they needed to.

Their argument last night about their new companion was forgiven; Willowvine didn't hold a grudge more than a few minutes. He would observe this Cornflower with care. Willowvine trusted too easily even though she had little faith in her ability. There was no proof Zerenia knew her, let alone made the referral. Springheart knew appearances could be manipulated with little effort.

Tom passed him a heavy bag to attach to the ring on the bottom of Blaze's saddle. "It contains the herbs and potions Dawnriver suggested," he said. "If it's too much, we can leave some."

"Are you trying to avoid learning?" Springheart asked. It would be a surprise if he said yes. The boy had been excited at the idea of becoming a healer only a few days ago.

"No. I just think he's gone a bit overboard. The more we put on the horses, the harder the ride."

"You don't trust him," Springheart said. "I understand given what happened, but you can trust that Zerenia did her diligence before suggesting him."

"Yes, I suppose. But he's not here and we need to go soon."

Dawnriver had agreed to meet them at the stables early enough to allow for a full day's travel. He'd mumbled something about a few errands when he woke. "There is still time."

Tom grumbled something and then went back to checking another horse's legs and hooves. Springheart doubted the animal had injured itself in the last few minutes, but it seemed to give Tom comfort.

An elf in dark cloak and travel clothes strode into the stable. "Stable master? I am here with your money."

He was older than Springheart, but that would only be evident to another elf. His hair streamed unbound behind him as he moved through the stable, calling out for attention. Both his look and behavior were unusual in Springheart's experience, unusual enough to make him cautious and curious. In the back of his mind, he heard Zerenia's warning to beware the fair and helpful. This stranger definitely fit the first part. There was a wild beauty to him.

Willowvine glanced up, as had most people at the interruption. She moved to stand near the stable master, as if she thought he needed protection.

"Ah, Needleblade," the master said. "You are here to settle the bill?"

"Yes, and I need a horse for the next leg of my journey. A fast one, if you please."

"You have the tariff?"

Renting a horse was usually a simple matter of exchanging contracts. This Needleblade must have a reputation for not paying if he was expected to do so up front.

"Yes, as we agreed. Now, which of these animals is my steed?"

The stable master held out his hand. Needleblade placed two small pouches in the palm. After counting the coins, the master nodded and gestured to a boy. "It will be a few minutes, unless you wish to ready him yourself?"

"I will wait," Needleblade said with a shocked arrogance at the idea he would stoop to such labor.

Springheart checked the cinches and clips as he watched Needleblade look around. The elf's eyes lighted on Willowvine, who had returned to her task. A smile crossed his face.

As if she'd felt his gaze, she turned from her task. "A good day to you."

Springheart tied his horse to the rail and moved onto Willowvine's, Hunter. The pack animal shifted weight and huffed as Tom moved on to saddle his own horse.

"It looks like you are also preparing to take a journey."

"Yes," she said.

Springheart knew her well enough to hear the dismissal in her tone. It made him both proud and hurt to see she had learned caution and didn't always need rudeness. Perhaps, the next thing she no longer needed would be him.

"I will be traveling alone," Needleblade said. "Toward the university. I am called to teach there."

"An honor, I think," she replied.

Hunter snorted, and Springheart realized he'd stopped brushing as he listened to the exchange.

"Yes. And may I be so bold as to ask your destination?"

Willowvine glanced at Springheart. He focused on the horse, moving the brush slowly along its flank. When he looked back up, she was lifting the pack.

"We are not leaving until our final companion arrives. I would not wish to inconvenience you for the benefit of company," she said. "I'm sure the master at the university is eager for you to arrive."

"Of course, but I would be willing to delay a little for the joy of riding with such a lovely young elf."

Springheart waited for her to announce her status as an orphan, something she did to put people off.

"Kind of you to say," she said. "I do not know when our companions will arrive."

SHE DIDN'T WANT to trust this elf who had appeared out of nowhere. He had too many questions and too willing to change his plans to accommodate them. She didn't want to be rude — she was trying very hard to portray herself as a civilized elf, but it wasn't working. Perhaps accepting Cornflower had used up her trust in strangers.

"Springheart," Willowvine called. "Are you busy?" If she could pass this off to Springheart, then she could observe what he did so she'd be prepared next time.

"Grooming Hunter can't wait," he said.

So, now she had a decision to make. Be rude and try harder the next time the opportunity arose, or dodge the situation and agree he could join them. There was always the hope that Dawnriver and Cornflower would be so late that Needleblade would give up.

"I think I can wait a little," Needleblade said. "It would be safer for me to travel with a group than on my own."

"Are the roads dangerous?" Willowvine knew they were not, but now she wondered how it would feel if she sent him on his way only to discover him injured when they passed him later.

"More lonely than risky," he said.

She had to start packing the supplies onto Hunter and that meant ending this conversation no matter what she preferred. "If you wish to wait, I'm sure we can journey together."

"How delightful," Needleblade said. "I will wait in the yard so as not to be in your way. Do you not want a wagon?"

"We prefer to travel lightly," Willowvine said. The last time they traveled with a wagon, Waterfeather used it as his personal transport and it became a tool for him to delay their progress more than an aid in carrying supplies.

She turned back to the task at hand, taking the now packed saddlebags to Springheart. "What did I do wrong?" she asked.

"How do you mean?" He adjusted the tack to accommodate the sacks holding their supplies, bags not needing the protection of the leather saddlebags.

"I know you were listening," she said. "I tried to be polite, but he didn't take the hint."

Springheart chuckled and she felt her temper rise.

"You were practicing for your reentry to Elven society?"

"I was trying to be civil." She snapped the words. "You said I need to do that to fit in."

He glanced at her and must have seen the anger in her eyes. "You did fine. He wasn't going to take no as an answer. Being civilized takes two people. The fault was his."

"Oh, but he's a scholar." She tied the leather strap to the saddle.

"It's acceptable for you to just say no if you don't want to do something," he said.

"I figure I need way more practice at civility before I try that." She picked up the next set of bags and headed to where Tom stood talking to the pack horse.

"How long are we going to wait for Dawnriver and the girl?" Tom asked. "I don't know about this Cornflower, but he can't just wander in when he feels like it."

"No longer," Dawnriver answered. He'd entered the stable and joined them without Willowvine noticing.

"I'm here too," Cornflower called from the entrance. She held the reins of a black mare.

"Get your horse ready," Willowvine said to Dawnriver. "We'll leave as soon as you're done."

"I've done it," Tom said. "Her name is Evenlight. You just need to attach your belongings. Give me anything bulky and I'll tie it onto Triumph here."

Needleblade waited for them at the entrance to the stables standing beside Cornflower, who glared at him.

If she doesn't like him, then we need to be more diligent. It's feeling like everyone has two jobs. Find the Stone and watch a companion.

"So, we are off," Needleblade said. "Perhaps we should pause to introduce ourselves."

"We can do that on the road," Willowvine said. "It's getting late and I want to make progress today, so our journey tomorrow is short."

She rode past Needleblade. He pulled in between her and Springheart. She reminded herself that not all strangers were enemies. And that the last time they harbored an enemy she thought he was a friend to start with. And that Zerenia's warning couldn't have possibly meant all their companions could not be trusted.

"WE HAVE BEEN on the road all day," he reported.

Rainblossom wanted more than travel progress. "Have you found a weakness in the girl?"

"She is holding something back, but I have yet to discover it."

"And what did you find about their search for the Stone?" She knew it was too early for that. Her spy was instructed to be subtle and if at all possible, garner the information while misdirecting the search. Early or not, she needed to keep him uncertain about his fate.

"I engaged in conversations with all of the team," he said. "The boy is more interested in the animals. He trusts only Willowvine and Springheart without question."

"The human boy may be the way in. They tend to be weak and greedy," Rainblossom said. "Find a way to win his trust."

This spy came highly recommended. She didn't doubt he was a devotee of the Society, which meant he would want the Stones of Power to remain hidden, or the last one at least. She doubted his ability to act quickly in the event that things changed, though. He appeared more comfortable following her orders to the letter than thinking for himself.

"I will find a way," he said. "I think Willowvine might not have shared the details with anyone other than Springheart. She is not one to trust a virtual stranger."

"Don't give me excuses," she said. "I want the location of the Stone and you will find it. Waterfeather damaged our chances, but it's still possible to complete our vision."

"And if I must harm her, or one of the others?"

Rainblossom preferred to keep her involvement secret. The Society was supposed to be dismantled after the disaster Water-feather caused. No one knew she was the leader. Violence against anyone connected to Willowvine may eventually bring notice. The girl might be an orphan, but she'd gained the attention of the Council.

"That will be the last option you take," she said. "What of the other?"

"He is merely an add-on to the group like me. He will not have any of the information we seek."

He was about to say something more, but she cut him off.

"Can you force him to leave the group?"

"He is persistent." The spy checked something in his hands. "If I could take more permanent measures?"

"No." She wasn't ready for that. "Continue to edge him out. I'm sure someone of your reputation will succeed." He didn't notice the sarcasm in her voice.

If the Stone of Orphan was found and replaced, her position would collapse. With all three Stones back in the maze, the elves would be strong enough to rule the whole world. The reason the Society formed in the first place was to prevent that very situation. The elves in control of the world would lead to war and suffering. War would break out as internal factions vied for supremacy. Or as other species felt more threatened. Peace was fragile without some threat backing it.

"You have time," she said. "It is best to isolate Willowvine first and then obtain her trust. Do nothing to turn her against you."

"I must return to the camp," he said. "They were suspicious of my leaving. I am supposed to be gathering firewood. But there is —"

Rainblossom ended the communication spell and went to stand at her window. The view was fitting for her status, both the public and private one. Her room in the tower rose high enough to allow her to see over the ancient trees of the university all the way to the mountains that separated the mainland from the port. If she could find a far-seeing spell, she would be able to watch the progress of Willowvine's team. She would be able to give her spy better instructions.

This place was too far from them. It was time to leave. She would go on a pilgrimage. No one needed to know that it was to find and destroy the Stone of Orphan.

Chapter 7

Willowvine poked at the fire, trying to get enough flame to cook their meal. They'd stopped early for the day, but now she worried that there wasn't enough wood available to keep it going through the night. "Isn't there a village close? We can't camp here if the supplies are so scarce."

"I'll get some more wood," Tom said. "It would be a pity to waste time breaking camp now that we're set up." He ran off before she could answer.

"Maybe Dawnriver and Needleblade had more success," Springheart said as he measured grain and herbs into the pot. "It's odd there is so little wood in the area."

"Other travelers have been here," she said, pointing to the charred patches where other fires had been doused. "It's the wrong time of year for the trees to drop branches."

"I know all of that," he said. "It still should be enough for three people to collect faster than this."

Dawnriver and Needleblade were both still looking for wood. Cornflower had stayed in the camp and was checking the tents.

The men's absence irked Willowvine. It was a convenient

excuse to leave the camp. On the last quest, Waterfeather had hidden his true agenda by doing a similar thing. The only difference was that he didn't offer to gather wood or bring water. His excuse was that he needed to meditate.

"It's not the same," she said. "You keep telling me to put the past aside, and I need to trust people."

"Yes," Springheart said. "I was only observing the facts, not accusing anyone."

She was close to doing it. "If they aren't back before Tom, we'll need to go find them. Neither of them looked prepared to travel, even though both of them claimed to be experienced."

"And you think we should be stealthy? Creep up on them to see if our worry is justified?"

She laughed. "I'd prefer to know they are trustworthy rather than just hope it."

"Caution is not distrust," Springheart said. "If you need to search for them, I can tend the fire."

"I'm trying to be trusting. It won't help if I keep spying on people who I've accepted as companions."

"And it would do no good for Tom if you reinforced his mistrust."

"Yes, that too." Willowvine smiled as she prodded the few sticks again. "Should we be doing more to get him comfortable with Dawnriver? Needleblade will be gone soon, but Tom will struggle to learn from someone he won't trust."

"Not yet," Springheart said. "Let Dawnriver win him over with his healing skills." He scanned the small clearing. "Here come our companions."

Willowvine looked up. Tom and Dawnriver, laden with small branches and sticks, crossed the clearing. Needleblade appeared to have been foraging in a swamp, but he carried a substantial log that would keep warm until morning.

As she watched, Tom laughed at something Dawnriver said. Then he turned to Needleblade and asked him a question. Needleblade looked down on Tom. His reply added to the boy's amusement.

When they joined her, Willowvine fed the small sticks to strengthen the fire before adding the log.

Cornflower joined her and sorted the kindling. "This isn't enough," she said.

Willowvine didn't answer, she fed the fire a few more twigs and then reached for the log. It was wet, not damp on the outside, which could be stripped, but soaked as though Needleblade had rescued it from a lake.

"Take down the tents," she said. "We'll go on to the village."

Cornflower smiled as though she'd won a prize. "A warm bed will be welcome."

"We might be forced to sleep in a barn," Springheart said. "But I think that would be an improvement on this camp."

The village was an hour off the road. Willowvine battled her anger at the detour, trying to find a little consolation in the idea of a hot meal and a dry bed.

"The others are upset with you," Cornflower said as she nudged her horse to ride beside Willowvine. "You made the right decision."

"They're not angry," Willowvine said. "Just quiet."

Cornflower didn't take the hint. "Then we must entertain each other," she said. "We should be friends. Tell me about yourself."

"There is nothing to tell," Willowvine said. Her past was hers to hold.

"I understand," Cornflower said. "I know what it is to be an orphan. With no one to care for you. The world is a cold place for us." She sighed and then smiled at Willowvine.

"The world is what you make it," Willowvine said. "I have friends. I always found people who cared about me."

"Friends are not the same as family," Cornflower said. "Friends come and go. Family is always constant."

"Until they aren't." Willowvine turned in the saddle to take a long look at Cornflower. How could she think that family was so constant? Orphans knew better than anyone how fragile they were.

A flash of something hard crossed Cornflower's face. "Yes, until they aren't able to be there. Our families didn't exile us. They didn't leave us voluntarily. Friends walk away when it's convenient."

Willowvine flushed with guilt. Cornflower couldn't have known how she left her gang, could she? "Sometimes when they have no choice. Sometimes to protect friends, you must leave." It sounded hollow.

"I know what it is like to have a family," Cornflower said, wistfully. "My relatives died in service to the Council. But that didn't mean anything when I was alone."

"All of your relatives?"

"It doesn't take a crowd to make a family. My mother and father and grandfather died in the last battle at the Well."

"A long time ago," Willowvine said. "You look so young."

Cornflower flushed.

Did I catch her in a lie?

"The battles were kept secret. There was one only twenty years ago. You would not have known. I was only two. Old enough to know the love of my parents."

"My mother died in childbirth," Willowvine said. "My father died before her." She didn't know more than just the bald facts. For most of her childhood she'd felt shame her life had come at the cost of her mother's. So much so that she'd concocted multiple lies about how she became an orphan. Why she felt Cornflower deserved the truth was a mystery.

"See," she said, "you don't understand what you are missing. I know what it is to be part of a family, accepted in the community. I know what I am missing."

"I pity you," Willowvine said. "I only know people who loved me without the obligation." She nudged her horse into a canter and left Cornflower behind.

TOM GLANCED AT TRIUMPH. The pack horse was laden more than he'd first expected, since somehow Cornflower had found a reason to add her bags. Tom swore he would remedy that at the village. The elf was charming, and he couldn't deny she was pretty, but he also couldn't ignore Zerenia's warning about trusting people like her.

"What have you been doing these last years, Cornflower?" Dawnriver asked. "It is not an easy world for a girl on her own."

Tom listened to the conversation with no shame, hoping the answers to Dawnriver's questions could settle his own mind.

"I do fine, thank you," Cornflower responded.

Tom glanced at her. She didn't look like traveling had aged her.

"Have you found a place to stay?" Dawnriver asked. "I mean, you haven't been traveling non-stop since you became an orphan."

"You have family?" Cornflower asked.

"Yes."

"Then you won't understand."

"Willowvine?" Dawnriver called to bring her into the conversation. "Perhaps you would understand, or Springheart?"

Tom hid a smile. The more people Dawnriver brought into it, the more for him to overhear.

"It is different," Willowvine answered. "I can't explain it."

"So, keep your questions to yourself," Cornflower said, all the charm gone from her voice.

"I'm just being friendly," Dawnriver said. "I'm happy to tell you about myself. It's called conversation."

"It is unwelcome," Cornflower said.

"Really? You joined us for companionship, or am I wrong?"

"I joined your group to help," Cornflower's voice was almost a snarl. "Not to answer rude questions. Do you not believe me?"

"About what?" Dawnriver asked. "All I know is that you say you are an orphan and you have skills in research...and your name, of course."

"I don't need to prove anything to you," Cornflower shouted.

Tom looked back to see her face blazed and eyes sparking with anger. She had no reason to be so angry. Dawnriver might be persistent, but all she had to do was ride forward to be rid of him.

"Why are you so upset?" Tom asked. "Like Dawnriver said, we're companions on this trip, for now at least." He stared at Needleblade as he spoke, but the elf avoided acknowledging the fight. "It helps to pass the time, talking."

"I don't answer questions." Cornflower kicked her horse and raced ahead of them on the road.

"What did we do?" Tom asked.

Willowvine rode forward to take Cornflower's place beside Dawnriver. "Life is hard when you are an orphan. Springheart and I have been lucky. Before I met him, I was part of a gang of thieves. I've done things I'm not proud of and don't want to talk about. If I hadn't joined up with Springheart, I may have turned out just as scared as Cornflower."

"She's scared?" Tom asked. He watched as the others

drifted back to their earlier positions. He hadn't noticed how close they'd been riding. "She's scary, that's for sure."

"It's easy to push people away with anger when you're afraid. Trust is a risk; I know that." Willowvine kept her eyes on Cornflower.

"But you trust me, and Springheart," Tom said. "The others, I don't know about. But Cornflower reminds me of Zerenia's words."

Willowvine shifted in her saddle. "Sometimes trying to find the reality in a vision will push you to make mistakes."

"Then you don't think Cornflower could be a danger?"

"I didn't say that," Willowvine said. "I only know our party is full of fair and pleasant strangers."

"It would be nice to trust people to be what they say," Tom said. "Or at least be able to trust one of our new partners."

"They aren't partners," Willowvine said. "We'll know if they can't be trusted, but I'm hoping that will happen soon. It's tiring to suspect everyone."

Tom laughed. "At least I'm not the only one."

Willowvine let her horse slip back to join Springheart at the rear of their group. Tom stared ahead to see Cornflower in the distance, where no one could ask her questions. He stroked Beacon's neck. "If only people were as easy as horses."

Chapter 8

Willowvine handed the reins to the groom and stretched. The idea of a bath and a soft bed was more appealing after the ride than she expected.

Cornflower's attitude hadn't improved on the road. No one had made any effort to smooth things over with her, and she'd stayed far ahead of them until they reached the village.

"Thank you for taking my side," Cornflower said. She linked Willowvine's arm with her own and gave a gentle tug toward the inn across the square. "It sometimes feels like I'm the only one who knows how lonely it is without a family."

Uncomfortable with the intimacy, Willowvine freed her arm and increased her pace. "It might go better for you if you tried a little harder to be friends."

Cornflower sighed. "I do find that hard," she said, voice quiet. "If I knew something about the others, maybe it would help. I would have a way to start a conversation."

Willowvine came to a stop in the middle of the town square. Cornflower had no problem starting conversations when it suited her. Their introduction at Zerenia's inn had not been awkward. This change of mood worried Willowvine. Was

Cornflower putting on an act? If she was, why would she choose such a prickly one?

The girl was staring at the ground before her, shoulders slouched. Willowvine took her arm and started moving again. They were as alone as possible in a town square. Springheart and Tom strolled the market, checking the few open stores to see if there was something that would help them on their journey that could be bartered for healing, so they spent as little of their coin as possible. Dawnriver and Needleblade had gone ahead to book their rooms.

"When we are settled, try asking Dawnriver about his family. Don't make it sound like you are jealous. Being an orphan doesn't have to be lonely. If you try, you can find someone like Springheart, or like Tom. Companions who will make your life more interesting. Someone to adventure with."

"I don't know," Cornflower said. "Will he talk to me?"

Willowvine opened the door to the inn. "I'm sure he will, but if you are afraid of him, perhaps Needleblade will talk about himself."

There were three rooms available at the inn. Before Willowvine could suggest they all share the largest, Cornflower announced that one of them would be for the women. She would be forced to feign sleep to keep Cornflower from nattering or whining at her all night.

At dinner, Willowvine sat between Tom and Springheart, leaving Cornflower to join Dawnriver and Needleblade. She told herself it was to give the girl a chance to get to know the other two better, but she couldn't quite deny it was to avoid spending the evening with her as well as the night.

"Cornflower," Willowvine said when it seemed they would eat in silence. "You must have some interesting stories about using your skills. What's the most obscure thing you've found?"

"I worked with a Scree merchant almost a year ago," she said, brightening. "He was looking for an artifact that was buried under long years of legend and myth." She stopped to pick at the food on her plate.

Willowvine's stomach clenched at her words. The first of their quests was because a Scree merchant had stolen the Stone of Family. She sipped her wine, trying to get her words in order. "Can you tell us who the merchant was?" She felt Springheart tense beside her. None of the others knew the story.

"I keep my clients' identities secret," Cornflower said. She held out her mug for more wine.

Perhaps more will loosen her lips and cause her to sleep through the night.

Springheart poured. "That is admirable," he said. "We have that in common. As couriers on Lands Home we were obliged to keep secrets. Can you hint at the artifact?"

Cornflower smiled. She was more comfortable being the center of attention and didn't seem to mind any of the questions now.

Willowvine held her breath, waiting for the answer.

"It was a jewel," Cornflower finally said. "A blue stone with a legend of its own."

"The Eye of Cartref?" Dawnriver asked. "I heard a rumor that someone found it."

"Your sources are good. Rumors will always follow an artifact, but you will never see The Eye," Cornflower said. "The merchant stored it away. He said owning it was the pleasure, no need to flaunt his acquisition and perhaps entice a thief." She laughed. "Or, another thief." She looked directly into Springheart's eyes. "Think of what I could do if I had a partner."

Willowvine couldn't look at Springheart. If he wanted to leave, then she wouldn't stop him. If he was attracted to Cornflower's antics, she didn't want to stop him.

"Yes," he said. "My partner is always improving my skills. I wish you luck in finding someone."

Cornflower's face hardened for a moment before she turned a sunny smile on Needleblade. "You must have stories of your own to tell." She turned back to Willowvine. "See, I am learning."

The rest of the evening passed in what became a contest for who could tell the most hair-raising tale and convince the others it was true. Willowvine kept Cornflower's wine mug full and retired early enough to truly be asleep when her roommate returned.

RAINBLOSSOM FELT the pull of a spell. Her spy was reporting again. It was sooner than she expected. Perhaps he was more capable than he appeared.

She left the hall, where other councilors held conversations in small groups, and entered a room set aside for private conversations. She placed the ward to ensure no one would interrupt and settled on the velvet bench.

"What do you have for me?"

"I made no progress on Willowvine," he said. "Or perhaps I have made a little. We may be approaching friendship. All I can confirm is that I no longer feel like she suspects me."

She couldn't trust his feelings. "Why?"

"The other girl," he said. "She blundered a little. Willowvine has taken a dislike to her."

"What other girl?" Rainblossom struggled not to shout. Her spy was supposed to help her with the quest, not let things get out of control.

"I tried to tell you that last time I reported."

"What other girl?" His excuses bored her.

"Her name is Cornflower, or that is what she tells us." He paused as though waiting for her to praise him. "I wondered if she was another of your agents?"

Rainblossom remained silent, a tactic that had worked well

in the past. If she didn't speak, he would, and he would make assumptions. She needed more information about the stranger to make a decision.

"She is young, and I think she's a thief. She says she's able to find obscure clues to artifacts or some such." He paused and Rainblossom knew he'd learned her secret. She couldn't be away from the hall long enough to show him how patient she could be.

"What is her family?"

"She claims to be an orphan, but I don't believe her. So, she is not one of ours?"

Ours? Rainblossom held back a laugh. "Do you think she will be of assistance to you?"

"I don't know her well enough to say. She is cagey about her background. When asked her about her past, she stormed off rather than answer."

"If she's someone's spy, she is not good. Either she hasn't built her false identity, or..."

"Or what?"

"I don't like the uncertainty. You must get rid of her."

"You want me to kill her?" He sounded eager.

She hated to waste a possible resource. "She has traveled the roads before?"

He nodded.

"She's a thief?"

"According to the stories she tells, yes. She has no qualms about taking what she wants. But when she isn't entertaining us, she's closed about her past. It could all be lies made up in the bottom of a wine bottle."

Creative enough to cause him to doubt the truth. That would be an asset. "Make her leave the group," she said. "Send her to me."

"But that might expose me." He paled at the thought.

"True, if you are careless. But I have faith that you possess the finesse to enlist her to our aid."

"If she's already working for one of our enemies, or is telling the truth, she might choose to tell the others."

He wasn't going to be persuaded to take the risk without an argument. The more he resisted, the more valuable this Cornflower became. "You must create a situation that isolates her from the others. When that is done, tell her nothing about our purpose, only that I will help her if she is willing. If nothing else works, tell her there is money to be gained."

He nodded. "I think money is the best way to tempt her. It will take some time to do this properly."

"Do it before you reach the university. If she is what she claims to be, we cannot risk her finding the location of the Stone."

"Very well," he said.

She raised her hand to end the spell and then remembered that she'd have known about Cornflower earlier by exercising a little patience. "Is there anything else?"

"No. I will report again when I have news."

"It had better be that the girl is on her way to me." Rainblossom ended the spell.

Complications were not welcome in her plans. The only bright spot in her day was that Willowvine faced the same obstacles without the benefit of distance. Rainblossom would make sure that stayed the same. No matter what happened on the quest for the Stone of Orphan, Willowvine would always be at a disadvantage.

THEY MET for breakfast in the common room of the inn. Cornflower looked fresh despite her drinking the night before. Willowvine wondered if one of her obscure clues had led to a hangover cure.

"We'll move on after the meal," Willowvine said, her voice low. The common room wasn't crowded, but a few strangers sat at a nearby table.

"We should ride together again," Cornflower said. "I prefer talking to you more than being questioned by the others."

Willowvine couldn't understand why Cornflower was trying to separate them. The others were right to ask questions about her. It only made Willowvine feel protective of them — even Needleblade, who she thought of as an intruder to their quest.

"We'll set up in a different order," Willowvine said. She nodded to the other members of their company as they came toward the table. "I'll take the lead, or the rear depending on Springheart's preference. We need to speed up a little."

Cornflower looked at the plates of food on the table and then chose a few morsels.

"You'll need more than that," Willowvine said. "I'm not stopping for so many rests today."

She took a few more nuts and a heel of bread.

When they were all sitting and had tea and food, Needle-blade placed a slim book on the table.

"I wonder if you can show us your skill," he said. "There is something in this book about an ancient secret. Perhaps not relevant to their quest, but it will be... helpful to see your skills are real."

"An excellent idea," Dawnriver said.

Willowvine waited for Cornflower to argue with Needle-blade, but she reached for the book without responding to his implied accusation.

"It would help if I knew what you seek," she said. When Willowvine didn't respond, she placed her hand on the cover. "I usually don't need much time, but this test may delay us."

"If you are taking too long, I'll say so." Willowvine wasn't letting this opportunity pass.

Cornflower nodded and closed her eyes. She stroked the

cover of the book and muttered words that Willowvine couldn't hear enough to understand. After a few minutes, Cornflower opened her eyes. "Are you sure it contains a secret? One that you can't uncover?"

Needleblade nodded. "Some of the passages hint at something, but then I can find no concrete information."

Cornflower grunted acknowledgment and then reached for her bag, pulling out a small wooden box. "This helps me when the secret is buried deep."

She opened the box and dabbed her fingertip into an orange powder. Rubbing the tips of all her fingers together spread the stain. She tapped on the rim of the box, letting the excess fall inside. With her clean hand she closed it and replaced it in her pack.

"The dye will not permanently stain the book," she said. Then she painted the edges of the pages with the smear of powder. "It will fade by the end of the day."

When the powder covered all the edges, like the gilt on some old human documents, she closed her eyes, cradling the book edge up in both hands.

She started muttering again. Willowvine kept her eyes on the book. The color of the dye faded. She leaned in closer and realized it was crawling onto one page. The skin on her nape prickled. This was unfamiliar magic.

Cornflower stopped speaking and opened her eyes. "We know where the secret lies, now I just have to winkle it out."

She took less time than a sip of tea.

"Here," Cornflower said. "There's an artifact hidden nearby. A village, only a few hours ride. I'll be able to locate it exactly when we arrive."

Needleblade took the book back and scanned the page. "I see nothing here."

"That just proves my skill," Cornflower said. "Could it be something that assists you?" she asked Willowvine.

Springheart answered. "We don't know unless you can tell us what this artifact is."

"I am only sure there is something there."

"How do we know you aren't telling us a lie?" Tom asked. "If we go to this village, it's at least a day's delay."

"Did you learn the location of the village in the book?" Dawnriver asked. He was the only one who didn't load his voice with accusation.

"I read 'In Garden's Rest a powerful thing protects the world'."

"With no specifics, it's a risk." Springheart turned to Willowvine. "Your decision."

"I know we'll be delayed," she said as she sorted out her mind. "It's more than we had before. We should go."

Cornflower turned on the sunshine smile. "Thank you for trusting me."

"We'll only know if you are truthful when we get there," Willowvine said. "Eat. I'll pay our bill. I want to be on the road to Garden's Rest in half an hour."

Chapter 9

Tom wanted a break, but Willowvine feared wasting time with this side trip posed enough of a delay that she wouldn't spend more of it coddling the horses. She didn't use those words, but Tom knew what she meant. And she had a point, but well cared for animals wouldn't fail them if it came to a fight.

Triumph, the pack horse, carried more than before — again. Rather than each day reducing their supplies, it felt to him like it brought more. The pace wouldn't harm any of their animals, at least not yet.

"Tom," Cornflower called from behind him.

He turned to see her crowding Triumph to get closer. That was stupid at this pace. "Stay back," he said. "What do you want?"

"No need to be rude," she said. "Can't that beast drop behind you?"

"It's my job to take care of the horses." So far, leading Triumph had made it impossible for her to bother him. He'd noticed how she tried to pull the others one by one into a private conversation, all the while speaking loud enough to be heard by everyone. "You need to drop back before you trip over him."

"I think my horse is hurt," she said. "Look at his foreleg."

Tom saw blood, even though the horse didn't limp. The next resting place was too far to wait. He needed to inspect the wound closer in case it was serious. The grass on the side of the road may not be wide enough to camp, but there was so little traffic he thought it would do for a quick stop. He called out to Willowvine, "We need a minute."

She grimaced, and he waited for her to say no, but she nodded and pulled to the side. "What?"

"My horse," Cornflower said, pointing.

Tom slid from Beacon's back and dropped the reins of both horses. As long as no one frightened them, the animals would stand and wait. "We can catch up if you don't want to stop," he said. "It's probably nothing."

Dawnriver dismounted. "I'll help."

"We'll all stay together," Willowvine said.

Cornflower remained in the saddle.

"Get down," Tom said. "If he's hurt, you won't be able to ride him."

She shrugged and slid to the ground. "How will I continue without a ride?"

Tom ignored her and joined Dawnriver at the horse's right foreleg.

"It's cut," Dawnriver said. "Not deep, but enough."

"No limp," Tom said. He put his hand on the wound, gently testing the damage. The horse didn't flinch, so he wasn't feeling pain. "It looks like a knife did this."

Dawnriver pulled a roll of cloth from his pouch. "Why isn't he hurting?" he whispered. "It isn't natural."

Tom rubbed his fingers together, the feeling dull and numb. "Malint sap. It couldn't have caused the cut, but maybe he brushed against a bruised leaf?"

Dawnriver glanced up at Cornflower and Tom followed his gaze. She looked at Willowvine, who was talking to Springheart and Needleblade. None of them shared his concern for the horse.

"She has a knife," Dawnriver said.

"You think she did this to slow us down?" Tom couldn't think of any reason she would resort to harming an animal for that.

"No," Dawnriver said. "Let's see what she does when we tell her the horse is fine."

They cleaned and wrapped the wound. Tom sent a little healing power into the cut, not wanting to drain his energy in case this was only the beginning of their problems. "You can ride," he said, holding out the reins to Cornflower.

"Are you sure?" she asked. "Perhaps I should ride with someone for a while. Give him some rest." She stepped close to Tom as she spoke. "Your horse could carry both of us with no problem."

Tom looked to Dawnriver for advice; he nodded once.

"Fine," Tom said. "An hour and then we'll see if there's more wrong than two healers could find."

They mounted, Cornflower behind Tom, holding tighter to his waist than he felt comfortable. Dawnriver took her reins so he could lead the animal.

Within minutes they were spread apart again. Willowvine ahead, Springheart behind. Dawnriver and Needleblade between Tom and Springheart.

"Now we can chat," Cornflower said, her breath warm on his neck.

"What about?" If he had to put up with her, then maybe he could find out why she was so determined to create problems.

"You travel rough," she said. "Can you not afford better? A carriage? An escort?"

"We travel light, not rough," Tom said.

"Are all your possessions on the pack animal?"

Did she think because he was young, he wouldn't figure out what she was up to? "Are all yours there?"

"It was nice of you to offer his strength," she said.

"Your bedroll and bag don't take much."

"Yes, but he is already burdened," she said. "I'm surprised Willowvine trusts all her valuables to one place."

"I'm not going to tell you what you want to know," Tom said. "You might as well keep quiet for the ride."

Cornflower laughed. "What do I want to know?"

"Where we keep our money."

"No, I was just concerned about the horse."

"Then you won't mind me telling Willowvine about your questions." He felt her stiffen. It strengthened his suspicions.

"I'll deny your accusations. Who would listen to a human when an elf speaks?"

"We'll see," Tom said. "Just be quiet until you're back on your own horse."

GARDEN'S REST turned out to be another deserted village.

Willowvine remembered the eerie feeling that she'd had when they'd been sidetracked under Waterfeather's direction. She really wanted to ride back out to the main road and head for the university, but that wouldn't be useful if they found another clue leading to this village and had to come back.

Dry leaves swirled around the horse's hooves as they trotted into the village. They stopped at what used to be an inn. The building itself looked as if it was ready for inhabitants, but the road outside was cluttered with litter. She dismounted and waited for the others to join her, hitching her horse to the bar outside.

"Do we search all of the buildings in this area, or do you have a clue for us to get closer?" Willowvine asked Cornflower.

"I'm not perfect," Cornflower said. Her smug grin said she thought the opposite. "But I think there are some likely places we should look. The oldest building in the village, and perhaps a place that might need protecting, like the barn or the well or something like that."

Willowvine shrugged. There were hours of light still left, and if they had to camp here overnight, it would not be such a heavy burden. The buildings seemed intact. They had their bedrolls, and it would be better than camping outside. Although, she would miss the starlight.

"I think we should split up," she said.

"I'll stay with the animals," Tom said.

"Needleblade and I can go looking for the oldest building," Springheart said.

Willowvine was glad that Needleblade would have someone with him who she could trust. "Dawnriver, why don't you come with me and we can have a quick look at the well? Let's all meet back here in about half an hour. I don't want us wandering around wasting time." She turned to Cornflower. "And what do you think would be most useful for you to do.?"

Cornflower looked around her and shrugged. "I am not very good at lifting stones or digging holes. Why don't I look after our packs and horses? Tom, you can go searching for the barn."

Tom looked at Willowvine, resentment at Cornflower's order plain in his scowl. Willowvine wanted the search over with as quickly as possible, and while she trusted Tom to go by himself, she didn't with the others. But then, how much damage could Cornflower do if left with their supplies, considering the well was only across the way.

"Dawnriver can go with you, Tom," Willowvine said.

She hurried to the well. It was a simple structure, a circle of stones built into a little wall and small roof set on top to hold the pulley. No ropes hung from the crossbar, and when she dropped a pebble inside, all she heard was a clunk as it hit the bottom. The well was dry; perhaps that's why people left.

She didn't know how best to check for the presence of an artifact. Even if that artifact was The Orphan Stone, how would she recognize it? She knew the general shape, but even the visible stones lost their individual shapes because of mortar and the shadows of other parts of the well.

She glanced back over her shoulder. Cornflower was sitting beside the horses, combing her hair. She looked around. Tom was walking towards her from a structure that looked like it had been a stable at one point. The others still searched the village. Willowvine waited for him to approach.

"Did you find anything?" she asked.

"Nope." Tom leaned against the low wall. "There was nothing that stands out to me as something important. Dawn-river is still looking."

"Maybe we should have seen if the book held more clues," Willowvine said with a laugh. "Let me just try using my magic. Perhaps something powerful will carry a signature."

She closed her eyes and tried to calm the voices inside telling her to pay attention to what was going on around her. She needed peace to read any aura. Tom could be trusted to bring her back to reality if there was a danger.

She found nothing in the well, so Willowvine let her magic drift away to its limit within the village. Mostly, things without life showed as a gray fog. She saw auras from her companions but didn't have time to go any deeper than noticing the bright-ness of the lights.

A warm glow that, if she remembered correctly, came from a side street, the one Tom searched earlier. She opened her eyes.

"Something is there," Willowvine said, pointing in the direction of the glow. "Will you find Dawnriver and look?"

Tom glanced over his shoulder. "You should know something about Cornflower before I go."

"I know she ordered you around, but she was right about the search."

"I think she wants to steal our money," Tom said. "She said some things to me today. You shouldn't trust her."

As if I need any advice on not trusting people.

"I'll keep my eye on her," Willowvine said. "But you and Dawnriver need to go look at that glow." She gave him directions and watched as he ran towards the side street.

She hadn't trusted Cornflower at all, but it was good to hear confirmation from someone else. Tom may be young, but he had a good sense of people.

Willowvine scanned the well one more time, still finding it empty of power. She turned to see Cornflower bending over their bags.

"What are you doing?" she yelled as she ran towards the girl. When Willowvine was only a few steps away, Cornflower finished digging in the bag and pulled out their money pouch.

"I'm not doing anything now," she said. "I have what I wanted."

Willowvine tried to dodge around the horses but Cornflower leapt onto the back of hers, picked up the reins that were just dangling on the ground, and smacked Triumph on his flank to cause panic.

The horses milled around, whinnying. The movement slowed Willowvine. As she pulled herself onto Hunter's back, she saw Cornflower cross the bridge to the main road and cut across open country.

She guided her horse from the churning pack and urged him forward.

Cornflower wasn't quite out of sight. Willowvine sped up,

hoping that her horse wouldn't stumble, and Cornflower's would.

The gap narrowed as Cornflower's horse started to climb the side of a hill. Willowvine urged Hunter forward, catching up. Cornflower was not as good a rider as she thought, thank goodness.

As soon as she came close enough, Willowvine pushed Cornflower from her horse.

"Just let me go," Cornflower said, scrambling to her feet. "You can always get more money."

Willowvine leapt to the ground and tried to pull the pouch from Cornflower's hands.

Cornflower grabbed a handful of grass and dirt from the ground and threw it at Willowvine, hitting her in the face, blinding her.

Willowvine refused to let go of the pouch. She didn't need sight to know that Cornflower was still trying to yank it out of her hands.

"Is this all you ever wanted?" Willowvine asked, hoping to distract her.

"Yes. You were stupid enough to think I was helping you?"

"Did you even have that power?"

Cornflower laughed and yanked one more time at the pouch, pulling it from Willowvine's hands. "How do you think I find things that I need?"

Still unable to see clearly, her eyes stinging, Willowvine stumbled forward to try to regain the pouch. Her fingertips brushed the leather, but Cornflower pulled it out of her reach. "Don't follow me. I'm letting you live — this time."

Chapter 10

Willowvine scrambled to her feet as she watched Cornflower mount the horse and dig her heels into his side. She ran for Hunter, scrambled onto the saddle, and urged him forward. The hillside was not a good place to gallop, and she knew that Tom would give her a lecture, or worse, be disappointed in the way she handled the situation.

Cornflower had pulled ahead of her and entered the edge of the forest. Willowvine couldn't let her get any farther away; she would lose her among the trees.

She entered the woods at the same place as Cornflower. Hunter refused to pick up speed and risk an injury. Perhaps that would help if Cornflower tried to force her own animal. The forest thickened only a few yards in, and here under the trees, it was cooler and darker. Willowvine listened for Cornflower's location.

The thump of hooves came from her right. Willowvine nudged her horse in that direction.

She heard the crack of a branch and a curse. She was glad her own horse had more sense than to run into a tree.

"Are you hurt?" She hoped Cornflower would respond and forget to worry about how it would lead Willowvine to her.

There was no answer.

The undergrowth parted moments later to show an animal trail that wound between the trees. She leaned against her horse's neck to avoid low hanging branches and urged him forward.

Another crack and then a horse whinnied.

Cornflower rode only a little distance ahead.

Willowvine didn't call out this time, not wanting to give away her location. She heard another thump; it told her Cornflower was only a few trees away.

She leaned back in the saddle to bring Hunter to a stop, dismounted, and tossed the reins over a branch. She checked her weapons, leaving her bow attached to the saddle and taking her throwing knives with her. If it came to a fight, it would be close quarters and a bow needed distance.

She crept towards the sound of a horse in pain. Willowvine stopped and leaned against the trunk of large oak. She rolled her body across the bark and looked ahead to a small clearing where Cornflower lay on the ground. Her horse struggled against a clump of undergrowth that tangled his feet.

"Be careful," Willowvine said. "He won't thank you if you hurt him."

Cornflower sprang to her feet, her hand going to the pouch at her side. "I told you not to follow me."

"We need that money." Willowvine wanted more than the pouch back; she needed to know if Cornflower was just a thief, or was she also a spy?

"I need it too," Cornflower said. "Everyone needs money. It's the only way to buy myself back into Elven society. I can't live like this anymore."

Willowvine knew the feeling. She also knew that money would not gain Cornflower entry to the community she craved.

"When I'm done with this quest, you won't have to buy your way in. Orphans will be accepted." She looked for an opening, a way to get the money back.

"You bought that?" Cornflower laughed as she clutched the pouch closer to her. "I'm not an orphan. I made a mistake. If I get enough money, I can buy my way back. Money makes people forget."

Willowvine tried to take in the fact that nothing about this girl was the truth. Am I so anxious to be accepted I'll believe anyone who is willing to befriend me?

"Who are you working for?" Willowvine took a half step towards Cornflower. She just needed to keep the girl talking. And she needed an answer.

"I'm not working for anyone." Cornflower backed up to where her horse now stood. The animal flinched when she touched his side but seem to have burned out his panic.

"So, you're just a common thief?" Willowvine took another step.

"Oh, I'm far from common," Cornflower said. She bent to untangle whatever held her horse's hoof; keeping her eyes on Willowvine the whole time.

Willowvine rushed towards her, counting on the fact that her reactions would be delayed by her task.

"Was anything you said the truth?" Willowvine snatched at the pouch, but Cornflower pulled it back toward her.

Cornflower's horse shifted position, nudging Willowvine to the side.

"I don't know what the truth is anymore," Cornflower said. "I don't care, either. Let me go. You have things to sell if you need more money." She freed her horse and mounted while Willowvine dodged the animal's flank.

Willowvine didn't have time to mount Hunter before Cornflower would be lost in the trees. She ran toward her as the horse dodged a downed branch, using the same obstacle to launch herself toward Cornflower.

Her hand caught the girl on her shoulder before she was secure in the saddle.

Willowvine landed on the ground beside Cornflower, rolling to hold her down. She couldn't let her run. Yes, they needed the money, but it was also about information. How had she been so gullible to let Cornflower join them? There had been so many hints at her nasty personality. Willowvine had felt kinship and defended the girl, but now she only felt stupid.

"Why did you pick us?" Willowvine asked as she pinned Cornflower at the shoulders. "We didn't look rich."

"You were just letting anyone join you. I watched you take that Dawnriver in and figured you might be an easy mark."

"We were expecting him." Willowvine tried to hold Cornflower down with one hand while she grabbed at the money pouch. Cornflower fought, unseating Willowvine.

Willowvine rolled back on top of Cornflower, pinning her again.

"Zerenia recommended him." Willowvine took a handful of Cornflower's tunic and tried to pull it tight to restrain her arms.

"Yeah. It was pretty easy to get the old lady to talk." Cornflower struggled against Willowvine's weight. "I told her I was meeting someone. I knew you were watching. She pointed me in the direction of the dining room. You made the rest of the story up in your head."

Willowvine hadn't even thought to confirm with anyone at the inn that Zerenia had recommended Cornflower join them. Surely one of the maids would have known something. In fact, she had no confirmation that Dawnriver was who Zerenia had sent them, either. She'd been so trusting, even through her constant suspicion of everyone.

"I won't trust anyone again." She grabbed for the pouch,

breaking the ties holding it together, but nothing spilled out. Cornflower still held the coin.

"Well, that's probably smart now that I'm leaving with your money," Cornflower said. "I mean, you've got two people traveling with you who you don't know at all."

"At least they didn't try to steal our money," Willowvine said, giving a final yank to the money pouch, tearing it from Cornflower's fingers.

Willowvine heard branches breaking and then Springheart calling her name. The others were too far to help, but all she had to do now was hold Cornflower here until they arrived. They wouldn't lose their money, and Cornflower could be taken to a constable.

"I don't know what you're looking for," Cornflower said, reaching for the pouch. "But you need to get hardened up. If you don't, you'll never find it. This world isn't kind or fair."

Willowvine opened her mouth to answer, to argue. She knew so many people who were fair, and kind, and helpful, but she felt Cornflower wiggle under her hips and tug on the pouch. Then a sharp heat in her side. She looked down. Blood soaked her tunic.

Cornflower laughed. "You can't even keep your head in the game with a fight," she said.

The heat from her body leaked out with the blood. Dizziness threatened Willowvine's ability to keep fighting. She tried to pull the pouch back from Cornflower, but the girl tipped her onto the ground and ran to her horse. Willowvine struggled to gain her feet, but weakness robbed her of the ability. No matter how much she wanted to get the money and bring Cornflower to justice, she could do nothing to stop her.

Cornflower mounted, stuck the pouch inside her tunic, and tightened her belt to hold it there. She turned to look at Willowvine. "Don't forget that everyone has a knife hidden somewhere." She snapped the reins and kicked the side of her horse, and within moments she disappeared from view.

Willowvine tried again to struggle to her feet as the sound of the others got closer; the effort increased the spinning in her head.

"I'm here." In Willowvine's mind it had been a shout, but she barely heard her own words.

They'll find the horse, and then hopefully me before it's too late.

She struggled to sit up, fighting the vertigo threatening to overwhelm her. She dragged herself up, lying on the branch she'd used as a springboard earlier. Blood still oozed between her fingers no matter how hard she pressed them on the wound.

Soon, Tom's healing powers would have no effect.

The others called.

Willowvine tried to answer but forming words seemed to take too much energy. It was getting hard to keep pressure on the wound with her hand as she felt consciousness slip.

Then she felt the vibrations of running feet as the voices became clearer.

"Over here," Dawnriver called.

A shadow darkened her fading vision.

"Let me get at the wound," he said. "You can let go. I need to touch you to heal it. Tom, help."

Chapter 11

Willowvine opened her eyes to see the clearing still around her. She looked down at her side. The bloodstain on her tunic had stopped spreading. She was weak, but no longer dying.

She sat up and looked around. The others had set up camp in the clear area where she'd first found Cornflower. She could see water containers sweating in the heat from the fire, the bedrolls arranged in a circle around the flames. Her mouth was dry, and not just because of the injury. She'd been so stupid, and it had almost cost their quest.

She struggled to her feet and joined the others at the fire. "Thank you. I'm sorry, I should never have let her do that."

Tom handed her a mug of tea and a full water-skin. "You can use this to clean your tunic," he said. "The food will be ready in a few minutes. You need to eat as much as you can manage. Your energy should come back. I'm sorry it took us so long to get here."

She touched his hand in gratitude. She had other tunics to wear, but this one was her favorite, and leaving it here for the flies would have hurt. "She took our money." Saying much more felt like too enormous an effort.

"We've worked with no money before," Springheart said. "I'm glad you're alive. We wouldn't have been able to go on without you."

"Remember what Zerenia told us," Tom said, keeping his voice quiet. "I think she meant Cornflower. I never met anyone so pretty and seeming so nice, and so horrible inside."

The guilt of ignoring the warnings overwhelmed Willowvine. She felt tears sliding down her face. It was weakness from the loss of blood, she told herself. "I'm sorry, I need to be smarter about this. There are too many people who are not what they seem in this world." She kept her eyes on the ground, deliberately not looking at either Needleblade or Dawnriver.

"And there are many people in this world who are exactly what they appear to be," Springheart said. "You'll feel better with food in your stomach. We'll spend the night here and be on our way in the morning."

"And the girl?" Needleblade asked. "Are we sure she's gone?"

"I think she spent enough time searching our belongings to know that the money was the only thing we had she could use or sell," Willowvine said. "Some of our things are only valuable to us."

"I have some money, if it comes to that," Needleblade said. "I'm sure I can pay for a few meals along the way."

"I have a small number of coins, too," Dawnriver said. "But we can also sell some of the healing herbs. Tom and I can trade our skills for a roof over our heads or a stable for the horses."

Willowvine chewed on the porridge of nuts and grains that served for her dinner, trying to keep her tears inside. Perhaps Springheart was right; here, two strangers offered to help, and she should learn to trust that.

"I think we should move as fast as possible for the university," she said. "We'll find a way to pay you back if we need to spend your coin." She rubbed her eyes as weakness overwhelmed her again. "Thank you. Did you find what was hidden at Garden's Rest?"

"Not our Stone," Springheart said. "A cup; we left it there. I suppose we know it means she didn't lie about her power."

WILLOWVINE HAD ARGUED about taking another rest. She wanted to reach the university as soon as possible. The teas Dawnriver and Tom forced on her were bringing back her stamina. And if she could keep going, then the others should be able to. She suspected they were pretending to need a rest for her sake, but she couldn't let them think she was weak.

The last two days had dragged on her as a series of bad decisions and useless efforts. It was there, at the university, that the real quest would start. She knew they would find some clue, some hint at where the Orphan Stone rested. And perhaps something to send them anywhere but to the Library at the Center. It sat too close to the Well for her to feel safe.

The horses couldn't be tired at the pace they'd been traveling, but Tom had insisted on a gentle start to make sure of the animals' stamina, or at least that was his excuse. When Dawnriver agreed with Tom, it seemed foolish to argue with two healers.

She took comfort in the knowledge that they would be at the university by dinner. There would be no further delays, and she wasn't letting anyone wander off. This stop would not take long.

"Let's take our meal by the river," she said. "It will be cooler, and we can all watch the horses."

"Good idea," Needleblade said. "I have an excellent trail food to share. A most nutritious and flavorful blend of dried fruit and raw nuts."

She had to admit he was generous with his supplies and seemed to know exactly what food would travel the best without being dried to the consistency of an old saddle.

They left the road at the entrance to a clearing. The elves maintained these rest stops for travelers. Always a clearing where fires could be set without risking the forest, always a river or a lake for fresh water. Most people left the clearing in the same condition they found it. The occasional party of Scree would leave their ashes and debris for others to clear.

She dismounted and led her horse to the river bank and watched the others. Tom and Dawnriver were in conversation about the animals. Tom seemed to have dropped his distrust of the older healer when the lessons started. She couldn't quite bring herself to do the same. It did not matter that she knew it came from past events, and that the feeling wasn't fair to their new companions. The suspicion would not go away. If she could use her magic, it might help, but her promise to stop reading people without good cause still held her back. Curiosity and paranoia were not good causes for violating someone's privacy.

"Are you going to glare at them all day?" Springheart asked.

Willowvine shook her head. It did nothing to dislodge her feelings. "I was thinking," she said.

"Of what?" Springheart handed her a small bowl of Needleblade's food.

She picked out some nuts and chewed on them while she thought about her answer. It would do no good lying to Springheart. He always knew when she did, and he'd nag her until she broke.

"I was thinking of using my magic on Needleblade and Dawnriver," she admitted. "Don't worry, I'm still working on proper behavior."

He chuckled. "There's proper behavior and there's

common sense. If you do believe they are not to be trusted, you should read their auras. Just the surface and no probing their secrets."

"But I thought you said it was rude," she said, stepping back into the shade of the willow behind them. The trunk and canopy of her namesake would support her as she focused on her magic.

"I trust your instincts," he said. "Just be careful not to get caught."

The likelihood of either elf being able to detect her was small. She'd come to realize that was what made her prying rude. People didn't want their secrets on display, and most people didn't harbor dangerous secrets.

"They are both busy," she whispered. "I'll do it now."

An arrow hit the tree six inches above her head.

Willowvine crouched and reached for her own bow, but it was still attached to Hunter's saddle.

Springheart had an arrow nocked and was seeking a target.

Needleblade scurried to hide behind a bush as another arrow dug into the muddy river bank.

Tom and Dawnriver held the reins of all five horses as they tried to pull the animals away from danger.

Three more arrows hit close by.

"There is more than one attacker," Willowvine said. She sank to the ground at the foot of the tree trunk. "I'll seek auras for you."

She closed her eyes and threw her senses out. "Behind the cluster of boulders on the hill," she said. "Two auras."

The vibration of hooves hitting the ground close to her dragged her back to the action. The horses passed only inches from her. "My bow," she said to Tom, holding out her hands.

In seconds she crouched beside Springheart. They crept to the edge of the willow's cover. Arrows still flew at them, but most hit the canopy of branches and lost momentum. Enough hit the ground in front of them to keep her and Springheart in the shadows.

"It's only two," she said. "I can get behind them if I circle around."

"I'll keep them there," Springheart said. "They chose that position because we can't shoot them, but they can't escape without showing themselves. Be fast, I only have so many arrows."

An arrow flew to Needleblade's hiding place, followed by a scream of pain. Another found Hunter's rump. Willowvine ignored the cries, trusting Tom and Dawnriver to deal with the injuries.

She slipped behind the tree and then ran to the closest cover. The attackers hid on the other side of the river, but they must be looking toward the willow where their targets took cover. They wouldn't notice her slipping across if she moved outside the angle of their aim.

She saw one of Springheart's arrows arc over the water and land on the boulder. It bounced off, but no answering arrow came.

She bent low and hopped across the rocks that narrowed the river only feet from the attackers. The pain in her side made it hard to balance with her bow in her hands, but it was not impossible.

Unless these attackers were elves, they wouldn't notice her until she was right on top of them. She took heart in the fact no arrows came her way.

A head popped up from behind the boulder. Human. He launched another arrow and Willowvine heard a curse. Another injury.

She braced herself to compensate for the dizzy breathlessness caused by her injury. She shot, and the arrow slipped between the two men. It should have caught one of them, but all it did was announce her presence.

The two attackers twisted to look, and one sent an arrow her way, it didn't even come close. They dropped out of sight.

Willowvine ran to their hiding place, pulling her knife from its sheath. Jumping into the shadow, she spun to attack. No one opposed her; the space was empty.

They were humans, so how did they disappear?

She shouted that it was safe so Springheart would come to her aid.

Spinning again, she found an opening. Just large enough a man could squeeze through. Springheart was wrong about the escape route.

She slipped inside. There was no scuffle of feet; the attackers must be long gone. A deep rumble caught her attention, making her step back into the space behind the boulder.

The rumbling stopped. Sand and dust billowed out of the hole.

"They blocked the passage," she said as Springheart slipped down beside her.

Chapter 12

Tom knelt beside Needleblade and let his healing power flow into the wound. The edges closed, and he could see the skin returning to health. Willowvine and Springheart were still not back and he wanted desperately to look for them.

"Don't strain it too much," he said. "You'll be fine in a few days."

Tom looked over to where Dawnriver leaned on Hunter's flank. As soon as the arrows stopped, Springheart had run toward the source, Tom and Dawnriver toward the wounded. He'd been surprised when Dawnriver had pointed him toward Needleblade. Tom was less experienced with humans; horses were his talent.

Hunter was resisting Dawnriver, and the healer didn't seem to know how to calm him.

"He won't settle until you talk to him," Tom said. "He's scared and hurting."

"I thought healing him would bring the calm," Dawnriver said.

"What about Triumph?" The pack horse had taken an arrow to his shoulder.

"I managed to hobble him. The wound isn't so bad."

Hobbling the horse was a good idea, but if the wound was minor, why hadn't he simply healed it?

"Let me show you," Tom said. He took Hunter's head gently between his hands. "It's me. Let us help." He whispered, knowing that it wasn't the words but the tone that would do the trick.

Hunter huffed and took a couple more paws at the ground, then calmed.

Dawnriver poured power into the wound, which sealed and left only a bare slice in the hair.

Tom turned at the sound of running feet. Willowvine and Springheart joined them, hardly even breathing hard.

Should he tell Willowvine about his suspicions? That Dawnriver might not be the healer he claimed?

"HOW LONG DO we need to stay here?" Willowvine asked as she watched Tom and Dawnriver tend to the wounded horses.

"A few more minutes," Tom said. "It's taking two of us. The horses are spooked, so they're harder to heal."

"Where is Needleblade?" she asked. "I don't want to delay our leaving to find him."

"I'm here," Needleblade said.

He walked toward them with a slight limp. She wondered how badly he'd been injured. From what she'd seen of his wound, the healing should be complete.

"Are you still injured?" she asked.

"Perhaps it's just in my head," Needleblade said. "The boy did a fast job."

"Tom?" Dawnriver called from beside Hunter, "I need your magic touch here."

Tom glanced at Willowvine and she almost asked him what

was wrong, but the call of an injured animal was stronger than whatever bothered him.

"The attack was such a shock," Needleblade said. "Are we safe on the road?"

Springheart left her to gather their belongings that had scattered when the horses panicked.

"The roads should be safe," she replied. "Perhaps things have changed. It is more important than ever for us to hurry to our destination. We need the latest news."

"Will the horses be ready?" Needleblade asked, taking a limping step.

"Yes," Willowvine said. She would not let this stranger impugn Tom's ability.

He took another step and winced.

"If you are in pain, speak to one of our healers." She pointed to Tom and Dawnriver. "We ride in a few minutes. I'm not stopping until we pass through the gates of the university."

She strode off to help Springheart retie the bags on the pack horse. There was no reason to think that Tom's power hadn't completely healed the man, and she had nothing more than a bad feeling about Needleblade to go on. Before she spoke to Springheart about it, she would need to observe and find a reason for that feeling or ignore it. She leaned toward the second option; he would not be their companion for more than today.

Springheart was searching the area where he'd piled their bags.

"What's wrong?" she asked, her mind occupied with her worries about Needleblade.

"Two bags are missing," Springheart said. "One had some extra clothing, but the other held Leafcreek's letters of introduction."

"Stolen?" She looked at the ground. It was smooth and clear where they stood, but the surrounding ground was churned by hooves and boots. The river rushed by only a few steps away.

"Or it went into the river," Springheart said. "We need to ask."

"And we need to leave before the attackers come back, or new ones arrive." Willowvine kicked at the pile of bags in frustration. They could continue without a change of clothes. The letters going missing could threaten their mission, now that they had so little money.

"We didn't get away unscathed," Needleblade said as he approached. He held out a sodden saddle bag. "I found this caught in the river bank."

Willowvine took the bag and looked inside. Clothing.

"We'll need to send a bird when we arrive at the university," she said to Springheart. "Let's get away from here."

THEY RODE as hard as Tom allowed them and arrived at the university just as the sun set.

Willowvine let the others arrange for the horses while she met with the head scholar.

"I'm afraid the person you were to meet will not be here until tomorrow evening," the elf said as he led her to a suite of rooms. "We have arranged accommodation for the others in your party nearby. These ones will give you space for study as well as rest."

"Thank you," she said. "We can't wait until tomorrow to start our research."

"I understand," he said. "Someone will be here after you've had time to clean up from your travels. They'll show you where to start."

The ache from riding so long warred with her burning need to find answers. Willowvine nodded and rubbed her hands on her trousers. "I need to send a message before I clean up," she said.

"If you like, I'll take the message for you."

How bad did she look, or smell? "Thank you." She wrote the message to Leafcreek and then headed for the baths.

THE WEARINESS SPRINGHEART felt from the day on the road and the attack waned at the sight of so many books and scrolls.

"Try not to take it personally," he said.

He worried that Willowvine's newfound civility only formed a thin veneer on her usual resentment of all Elven society. "He will arrive tomorrow, and at least we have access to the archives."

She grinned at him, and he saw his familiar cheeky companion in the expression. So many things were changing that it comforted him to know Willowvine was the same where it counted.

"We can start with the song," she said. "Maybe we'll find the information we need and can leave tomorrow after breakfast, without Needleblade."

"So, you have come to trust Dawnriver?" He couldn't argue with her feelings about Needleblade. There was something hidden in that man. Although he would bet money that Dawnriver had a secret, too. But he couldn't push aside the knowledge that elves worked that way. They kept things hidden simply because revealing them would cause pain or embarrassment.

"Tom doesn't, yet."

She stood in a small intersection of the long rows of bookshelves. The floor was decorated with a mosaic of musical notes. This was where the song was meant to be sung. A few repetitions of the seeking spell included in the music would light up any reference to what they needed.

"It seemed like Tom began learning to trust today, and then after the attack, he became distant from his tutor." Springheart pulled a scrap of paper from his pack and a pencil. "If he continues with this attitude, he won't learn."

Willowvine looked over his shoulder as he listed the specific terms to add to the spell. "We don't have time to find someone new," she said. "If we knew exactly where they were right now, I might be able to scan them."

"Too many auras?"

"Yes." She pointed to the end of the list. "Add myths and legends."

"Good idea." He made the notes.

"Before we leave then," he said, "it would be good to know if our suspicions were founded in something other than the lingering effect of our dealings with Waterfeather and his cult."

"That society may still exist," she said. "Let's get this done."

Chapter 13

His room was near the others, a blessing since he suspected they didn't hold him in high esteem. Being close meant they couldn't slip out and evade him. Having his own accommodation meant he could report in to Rainblossom as he saw fit.

Now that he wasn't huddled in a clearing, he could create a simple spell that would connect them through water. The element conducted magic well and could be manipulated to enhance a spell. Saving his energy for other uses allowed him to continue his deception.

He called Rainblossom's name on the still surface of the water and waited. Her response came slowly, starting as a swirl of red in the center of the bowl, although the water did not move, and then resolving into her face.

"Where are you?"

He wondered that she needed to ask. He had no doubt she had a tracking spell on him, if not on the rest of the group. "The university. Willowvine and Springheart are in the archives."

"Why are you not with them?"

"It would be too obvious, I think. But it matters not. I will stop them achieving their goal regardless of the information they glean."

Her image glanced over her shoulder. There was someone else in the room with her.

"Are we alone?" he asked, worried that she'd set another to his task.

"We are now," she replied. "Is your place on the team secured?"

He wouldn't lie exactly, but neither would he admit how shaky his position was. "It has only been two days," he said. "And the incident on the road today didn't help."

Her eyes narrowed. "What incident?"

"The attack," he said. "I assumed you arranged it to slow our progress."

"Did someone die?"

"We were lucky. A few injuries that our healers managed without too much effort."

"If I had arranged it, those two orphans would be dead."

Time to change the subject. Her threat against the orphans felt very much like it was turned on him as well. "Were you able to contact Cornflower? Is she helping us?"

"You do not need to know the whole of my plans."

Did they have another adversary? Or was she immersed in more than one plot? "Will you find out who did order the attack?"

"Perhaps it was only bandits," she said. "The road is a dangerous place."

He chose not to push for more. "We will be here until tomorrow evening at least," he said. "The scholar they wished to meet is away."

She nodded slowly and told him to wait. The water became murky. He glanced around the small room as he waited for her to turn her attention on him again. One window, a bed, and a table he could use as a worktop. The meals were all served in the dining hall. None of the scholars felt comfortable having food and drink near their precious books and scrolls.

He heard his name and cringed. If she took offense to his wandering, she would not be kind.

"I'm listening," he said.

"I believe the human boy is the weakest link. You should have no problems gaining his trust," she said. "Do not allow them to leave you behind."

She had not met Tom, he thought. The boy cultivated more suspicion than any of the elves in the party.

"I will find more interests that we share," he said. "Healing may not be the only passion the boy has."

"Report to me before you leave the university." She didn't wait for his acknowledgment.

He stared at the clear water in the bowl. It was difficult after these conversations to regain his amiable veneer. He would meditate on the vital nature of his mission.

WILLOWVINE FELT disappointed with the wait for the scholar, but he would be arriving at dinner, and she could do her own searching in the meantime. Their exploration in the archives was both fruitful and of no value, despite a night spent trying to interpret the information. There had been multiple responses to the song, but when they read the seven scrolls uncovered by the spell, the clue didn't shine from the pages. If only Cornflower had been an ally, the work might not drag so much on her patience.

Now, at lunch, with just their team, she was determined to set aside or confirm her suspicions about her companions. Needleblade was off settling into his new job and they would leave without him, so she concentrated on Dawnriver, who sat next to Tom picking at his plate of food.

He was amiable enough to be good company, an improvement on Waterfeather. But pleasant personalities didn't guarantee loyalty. If she could read his aura, it might help, but with so many people around, auras overlapped, and she couldn't find a way to sort through them.

"How is your training going, Tom?" she asked. "You had some opportunity to learn after the attack."

"I'm afraid Tom was the teacher," Dawnriver said. "My expertise is in people of all kinds. Tom showed me how woefully little I know of healing horses."

"You did okay," Tom said, not looking up. "Everyone got healed."

"No one can be an expert in every aspect of their craft," Springheart said. "I think it's good that Tom will teach as much as he learns."

"Indeed," Dawnriver said. "And your search of the archives? Did you make progress?"

Willowvine let Springheart answer, even though the healer looked at her as he asked.

"There were some results," Springheart said. "However, I think we still need a scholar to interpret. The spell does not distinguish between the clear and the obscure information."

The news didn't elicit a reaction from Dawnriver. Willowvine wasn't sure what she expected; perhaps surprise?

"Would you like me to look at the scrolls?" Dawnriver asked. "I may not be blessed with a gift, but I gained some ability in solving the convoluted hints our ancestors left behind."

"A scholar as well as a healer?" Willowvine asked. There was no way she would give Dawnriver access to what they'd found. His offer made her even more suspicious. Was he trying to misdirect them? To steal the clues and get to the Stone first?

"Perhaps," Springheart said. "I think we all deserve to rest until our meeting this evening. If we still need help, we will ask."

So, Springheart suspected him too. Willowvine relaxed. It was a relief to know she had company and it was not paranoia driving her distrust.

"It may be that your tiredness is stopping you from untying the puzzle." Dawnriver reached for the wine bottle. "Another glass will ensure a more restful few hours." He held it up and waited for them to nod before pouring.

"What is your plan to teach Tom?" Willowvine asked. "It must be a challenge to travel and provide the training he needs."

"If every day is like yesterday, there will be plenty of opportunity," Dawnriver said, laughing. "But I will not count on it. My plan is to first assess where Tom requires training, and only then fill the gaps. Don't worry, we have no plans to make you ill in order to practice healing."

"So, theory only?" Springheart asked.

"No, but theory is a good place to start." Dawnriver drained his glass. "I will leave you now. The wine has done its work."

When they were alone, Willowvine checked to make sure the door was locked. "Tom, do you not like your mentor?"

"It's hard not to like him," Tom said. "I'm just not sure if I trust him."

"Why?" Springheart asked. "Has he done anything to prompt your suspicion?"

"No, and neither did Waterfeather," Tom said. "Someone ordered that attack. And both Needleblade and Dawnriver left us the night before."

Willowvine leaned forward. Tom had voiced her thoughts. "Why would one of them order an attack that could have killed us all?"

"Well," Tom said, "maybe the attackers weren't professional. Only Needleblade got hurt badly. It was lucky we had two healers. Maybe his injury was to make us feel he couldn't have ordered the attack, or maybe Dawnriver knew he could deal with any wounds that happened. I can think of more."

He could put words to his worries, at least. "How are you so sure it wasn't just bandits?" Willowvine asked. Their mission would be threatened as much by unfounded mistrust as it would by a traitor.

"There were no other signs of violence," Tom said. "Bandits return to familiar territory because they get comfortable with the escape routes. I don't think it could have been one of their ambush points."

"What makes you think that?" Springheart asked.

"Sir Jode taught all of us kids to be safe on the road. He told us how to notice if something is wrong, and I didn't see any signs."

"It wasn't one of us," Willowvine said. "So, if someone ordered it, we can't rule out Needleblade or Dawnriver."

"We'll know when we move on," Springheart said. "Only Dawnriver will continue with us. Since he came with a recommendation, I hope he is not an enemy. That would mean we face other, more powerful ones who stay hidden, and that is cause for more than worry."

"We really only have Dawnriver's word that Zerenia recommended him." Willowvine emptied her glass. It was too late to check to see if a bird brought an answer to their message from Leafcreek. Perhaps when it came, she would know more.

"He was right about one thing," she said. "We need to rest." And I need time to try once more to glean something useful from the library.

.   .   .

THEIR SCHOLAR, Stonerose, was not what she'd expected. Willowvine looked at the elf who stood before her. He was young, and she'd imagined someone as old as Leafcreek. He was also rude, something she thought impossible in an elf of his standing. Perhaps Springheart was training her to become overly polite to make up for her lack of family.

"I said I would only speak with the orphans." Stonerose stepped aside from the door. "The others must leave."

"They are part of our company," Willowvine said. "They will learn what you tell us, so why not let them stay?"

"My agreement was to provide assistance to Willowvine and Springheart. No one mentioned a healer, and certainly not a human."

Springheart touched her arm. "We can't delay."

She felt tempted to send her magic out to test Stonerose's aura. Something stirred her anger and she wasn't sure why.

"We'll go check the horses," Tom said.

"And the supplies," Dawnriver said. "I sense we will want to leave quickly. No point in delaying to barter for essentials."

"They see the reason in my request," Stonerose said. "Why do you resist?"

That was a very good question.

She clamped down on the anger that refused to abate. "I am not. We should start with the scrolls we found yesterday."

When the door closed behind Tom, she moved to the table where Springheart had placed the materials. "They are supposed to contain clues, but we have not been able to decipher anything."

Chapter 14

Stonerose picked through the scrolls, scanning them quickly and then tossing them aside. "You may not have asked the right question of the spell." He didn't clarify what they should have done, just removed the bag he'd been carrying on his shoulder and started emptying it. "This is what I found, but not just in the archives. My colleagues had the documents in their rooms and private libraries. It is discouraged, but all too common."

"Someone else is looking for the stone?" Willowvine shivered at the thought of another seeker competing for the Stone.

"No," Stonerose said. "Or, at least as far as I know. These carry more information than what you seek and here, we research more than we eat or rest."

"That is good to know," Springheart said. "Our task remains urgent, but as far as we know, it is not a race against anyone."

Willowvine pointed to the table, which was now covered in papers and books. "Do these tell us where the Stone was hidden?"

Stonerose looked around the room. He went to the sideboard, poured a mug of wine and picked at a bowl of fruit and nuts. "Possibly, if we knew how to look for that information. But we suspect that the Stone of Orphan was taken by a cult, is that correct?"

Cult, secret society, whatever you called it, Willowvine knew they worked in the shadows. "Yes. We've been told that the society was rooted out. Do you mean that they would have recorded their actions?"

Stonerose chuckled. Willowvine tried unsuccessfully not to hear the patronizing tone. "If they are elves, they would have recorded everything. The question you should ask is, are their records collected in their libraries?"

"I think it has been too soon for you to have collected them here," Springheart said, "let alone study them."

"Ah, you are thinking of the most recent form of the cult," Stonerose said. "Those who took the Stone would not necessarily be the ones who now seek to keep it hidden. To protect the Stone from discovery, someone must guard it, or check that it remains hidden, so the location must be known."

"And you think you have the records from that time here?" Willowvine looked at the table. Nothing seemed old enough to contain what they needed.

"Here, or at the Library at the Center of the World." Stonerose placed the empty wine mug on the sideboard and rejoined them at the small table. "In this amount of time, I can almost guarantee the records found their way to a great library, and this one and the one at the Center are the oldest."

Willowvine heard real passion in Stonerose's voice as he spoke about the two libraries. His emotions added a softness to his character.

"How will we find what we need?" she asked.

"You must search through the whole library." He held out a slip of parchment. "I assume, however, that you have no time for that endeavor. So, I composed a more complex version of the catalog spell you sang."

Springheart took the scrap from him and tucked it into his pouch. "This could take a long time," he said.

"Perhaps not. I am about to take you to a place where you will find assistance. A place I could not reveal to your companions." His eyes gleamed with excitement. "Bring one of these documents to use for a demonstration."

Willowvine picked up the thickest book on the table, and one of the original scrolls.

They traveled through empty halls and down twisted stairs until they descended so far below the surface, there was no heat. The air was dry and had a slightly medicinal tang when Willowvine breathed through her mouth. She wanted to ask where they were going but Stonerose sped up as they went down yet another spiral of stairs.

"This is the lowest level," he said, stepping in front of a door carved with images of the journey of life from birth to death. "Our oldest documents are here for protection, some for repair. This is also where the newest acquisitions are brought for cataloging."

He placed his lantern in a niche in the wall, then pulled the doors open. Inside was lit by ettran stones, their glow illuminating the contents and decorations.

Bones, all bones. They were piled in pyramids of skulls, arranged in bouquets and scenes, and placed in glass cabinets with locks made of finger bones.

The air was dry and carried a faintly sweet scent. Willowvine stepped closer to Springheart as she tried to take it all in.

"I hope this doesn't disturb you too much," Stonerose said, striding to a cabinet and inserting a key. "These are the remains of scholars who die at the university. One day, I hope to rest here."

It wasn't upsetting, Willowvine thought as she gazed around, noticing that the ettran stones were contained in skulls and rib cages. "It feels reverential," she said. "I sense peace here."

She turned to look at Springheart. He was taking in the whole room just as she had.

"Yes," he said. "I feel that too."

Her attention was brought back to the scholar at the click of the lock opening. "We have artifacts here that contain spells laid after death. Some we no longer know how to cast. Some which are too dangerous to place on a living person."

He slipped on white gloves and took a small circle of bones from the case. Willowvine leaned over to see what it was. A crystal nestled in a frame of tiny bones. The whole device was attached to a handle made of a jaw bone. The crystal itself was clear, but Willowvine noticed a sheen on the surface that faded in waves from pink to blue.

"These are all bones from the ear," Stonerose said. "The spell requires something from the senses and there are no bones in the eyes."

He took another pair of thin cotton gloves from a drawer and handed them to her.

"And what will this do?" she asked, slipping the gloves on.

"Any document that you read through the crystal will reveal hidden truths." Stonerose took the book and scroll and placed them on a reading desk. "It will only reveal a few words at a time, but there will be no obscurity. When you see them, you will know the truth."

"Can we take this?" Springheart asked. "We will need to read through all the documents we find."

"Not from this building. It is too fragile to travel," Stonerose said. "There will be something similar in the Library at the Center of the World, but not in the smaller ones."

"Will we need to bring everything here to read?" Willowvine asked as she unrolled the scroll with one hand.

"I have received permission to allow you to use it in your rooms. You must not reveal it to anyone else. And it will be taken to and from your rooms by one of our scholars."

Willowvine passed the crystal over the flattened scroll. The device magnified the words, and the spell adjusted based on the length of the words to allow only four at a time. "We will need note paper," she muttered. Then her breath caught. The crystal displayed four words.

Orphan Stone is danger.

Chapter 15

Looking through the crystal hurt her eyes after only a short time. They'd taken turns at first. One reading out the words, the other writing them, and then Springheart called a rest. Willowvine had agreed but been unable to sleep. Now, two hours after Springheart left her to work alone, she conceded she needed a break.

What they discovered didn't stop her feeling they were missing a critical piece. They could only use the device while at the university, and it was the only way to read some of the messages. It was too fragile to steal and take with her, not that she hadn't considered it.

In addition to the strain on her eyes from reading, she worried because Leafcreek still hadn't responded. She tried not to dwell on the possibility he no longer lived. She believed she would know if that happened before they returned. A bird might easily meet with an accident, or many other things could stop the message arriving, hers or his. She could send another, but they wouldn't delay leaving to hear an answer.

Willowvine placed the bone and crystal tool on the soft

cushion the courier had used to deliver it. She straightened and felt her back twinge. She stretched, yawned, and rose to leave.

It was late and the corridors were mostly empty. She headed for the archives, thinking she would research the Library at the Center of the World. She'd been to that Library before, when they sealed the Well Between Worlds. But no one spared them time for reading. Almost right after they slew the beast, the council reminded them orphans were not welcome in the Elven lands.

A light shone from the archives. She stepped inside, hoping it didn't mean others were searching the same records.

"How nice to see you," Needleblade said. "I feared I would not get the chance to say goodbye."

"Are you leaving? I thought you were called to teach." One more worry to add to the burden. She'd hoped the question of his trustworthiness was answered. Well, knowing his schedule would help them avoid him. "Or did you mean when we leave?"

He held up a sack full of papers. "Like you, I have a quest. My masters charged me with seeking out new scholars. I ride out on my mission tomorrow. How goes your own quest?"

Her heart stopped for a beat. How did he know about the Stone? Then she realized he meant quest for knowledge. "Well enough, a little luck that raised more questions."

"Enough to help you on the next leg of your journey?"

"Is there ever enough when it comes to knowledge?" She wasn't going to tell him their plans. "Will you leave at first light?" They couldn't let him see the direction they took.

"I am not in such haste. I will likely rest until after lunch," he said. "Perhaps we can meet again?"

"Perhaps," she said. "There are still books to read, and my companions are not yet finished with their tasks."

Needleblade slung the bag over his shoulder. "I'll wish you luck and leave you to it."

She watched until he disappeared around the first corridor before singing the spell. She'd created it as she walked to the archive, adding words aimed at finding information on the Library at the Center.

All she found was a description of the building project, a list of the contents of the Library a hundred years out of date, and a floor plan. Willowvine copied the floor plan, thinking it would be the only helpful item on the list, and placed it in her pouch.

The research had done its job in making her sleepy, so she closed the door behind her and started toward her room. At the first side corridor, she heard familiar voices; Tom and Dawnriver whispering together as they walked. She waited until they were close before greeting them.

Tom smiled at her. "You should be resting," he said.

"And you," she said, yawning.

"We were called to attend one of the scholars," Dawnriver said as they walked together. "Stonerose fell ill shortly after returning to his chambers."

"What sort of illness?" Willowvine asked. Would it delay them? As soon as the thought formed, she felt shame warm her cheeks. People were ill. Not everything represented an attack on, or damage to, her quest.

"Nothing catching," Tom said. "Something he'd eaten caused the problem. He's fine now."

"Poison?" She struggled with the fear that someone was conducting a covert attack. "Because he helped us?"

"He has a weakness for certain foods he should not eat," Dawnriver said. "I believe it was an overindulgence this time. But we did not test for poison. Should we go back?"

It's paranoia, she told herself. "No. Rest and be ready to move on."

"I checked the horses and supplies earlier," Tom said. "We

can go whenever you need to. I'll just need a few minutes notice. Or I can get them ready to ride right now."

Tom's diligence made her smile. He'd appointed himself the guardian of their belongings and horses.

"I don't think they would like wearing their saddles for hours simply waiting to ride. You don't have to take on all of that, Tom. We should all be sharing the work."

"You won't let us help with the research," he said. "So, I look after the rest."

"When will we be leaving?" Dawnriver asked.

She wanted to tell them they would be leaving now, but there were still too many pages to read with the device. And she had no energy for the focus it required. "Our research hasn't given us all the answers, but it will be completed soon."

"And our destination?" Dawnriver asked.

"Perhaps it is better not to talk about that until we are on the road." She yawned again. "We all have time to sleep, don't worry."

"Then we will meet again over breakfast," Dawnriver said.

"Don't make yourself ill," Tom said. "You need rest. If we leave while you're exhausted, we might end up in more trouble."

"I will sleep," she promised. "There is more research to finish in the morning."

They parted ways at Willowvine's door.

"Three hours sleep," Tom ordered. "Minimum."

Willowvine laughed and agreed.

RAINBLOSSOM WAS REGRETTING ASKING her agent for frequent updates. Why was it so hard to find people for the cause who could make sensible decisions without close guidance?

"So, you have not yet found useful information," she said.

"We are at the university," he answered, annoyance creeping into his tone. "It is difficult to find time and places where we can talk enough about the mission."

It should be easier, Rainblossom thought. So many people around who could act as distractions or be bribed to give the information he needed.

"And your assumptions from what you observe?"

He didn't answer immediately. She sensed his fear at making a mistake.

"I have tried to align my own activities with those of Willowvine and Springheart, but they are isolated by the scholar. They disappeared yesterday and then locked themselves in their chambers with documents. Something arrived by messenger later. I managed to talk to Willowvine an hour ago. She was distracted. She would only let me know they needed to research more, but I think they are planning to leave tomorrow."

"Did she say that?"

"No. She was careful what she said about the future."

"Are you concerned they will leave without you?"

"I will be with them," he said. "I simply need to stay alert to their plans and remain useful."

She wondered how useful he was in truth. "See that you do."

He cleared his throat. "It would help if we were delayed," he said.

"You will be," she answered and closed the link. Finding Cornflower had been simple. Buying her loyalty was cheaper and faster than trying to indoctrinate her. The girl would stir up trouble and that was what would delay Willowvine.

Chapter 16

No matter how much she dug, Willowvine only found hints about the Stone. How had a secret society managed to hide all evidence of what they'd done with it? She could only hope that the Library at the Center held more details.

Leafcreek still hadn't responded to their message, and they couldn't wait any longer. At breakfast they'd decided to leave right after the meal. And so here she was, sneaking out like the old days when she was a courier. The thought made her smile, the old days were only a few weeks in the past.

The door to the courtyard where the horses would be waiting opened as she approached. Springheart held it for her. "There is a problem," he said.

"Will it wait until we are away from here?"

"We are not leaving," Springheart said. "The horses are gone."

She glanced toward the courtyard where their animals should have been waiting. Tom and Dawnriver were talking to the stable master, who was agitated and calling for the grooms to join him.

"Can we hire other horses?" she asked. "Why are ours gone? Do you mean they left? Or are they dead?"

"Someone came in the night and took all the horses. Ours, and everyone's. There is nothing to hire."

Willowvine glanced at the high walls and sturdy gate. "How?"

They reached the small group in the center of the courtyard. Another traveler had joined them. A Scree woman with all the rage of her clan on her face loomed over the stable master. Willowvine touched her knives, making sure they were ready if violence erupted.

"Do you not place wards on the gates?" the woman asked. "This would not happen in a Scree stable. Horses are too valuable."

"Yes. We had some security," the stable master answered. "This is not a place where we experience frequent bandit attacks. We will increase our spells when the replacement horses arrive."

"I cannot wait for you to find animals," the Scree said. "I go hunt the ones who stole from you. I will not return, but you can look for your horses if you wish. I will leave them hobbled where I find them."

"We will come with you," Springheart said. He turned to Willowvine. "We can bring the horses back and be on our way."

She wanted to help, but their mission was too important. "How long will it take to get these replacements?"

"A day, no more." The stable master pulled one of the grooms forward. "I already sent one boy to the village. This one will go now. I promise we will have what you need as soon as it is possible."

"What's all the fuss?"

Willowvine spun at the sound of Needleblade's voice. He'd

said he planned to leave later in the day, and it was only moments past dawn.

She let the others explain and drew Tom aside. "Will new horses be a problem?"

"I miss ours," he said. "I hope they come to no harm." He looked toward the gates. "I could go with the Scree woman."

"She will move far too fast for you to keep up," Willowvine said. "Will we be able to leave tomorrow with the new horses?"

"We'll check them over," Tom said, pointing to Dawnriver. "I'll make sure we take the best ones. But I think we should try to find ours."

Willowvine was torn. An extra day would give them a chance to research more but there was no guarantee there was anything useful to find. The delay would give her time to try to reach Leafcreek by magic; his silence still dragged on her heart.

She couldn't leave their belongings unguarded now. Yesterday she trusted her wards, but now that someone had intruded on the stables, she needed someone guarding them.

Racing around to find missing animals might also result in wasted time. It felt like she was trapped in a dream world where no matter how fast she ran, she stayed in the same place.

"If we find the horses, do you think we could ride out today?" she asked.

"It depends on how they were treated," Tom said. "We should try to find them though. I can't just leave them without trying."

She looked over to the gate. The Scree woman was adjusting her bags so they wouldn't impede her as she ran. Willowvine wanted to go with her, but she didn't trust Dawnriver enough to leave him here unwatched, and she couldn't risk sending Tom's teacher if bandits ranged the hills around the university.

"She's agreed to run with me," Springheart said, joining them. "I'll return by nightfall if we don't find anything."

"We'll be here," Willowvine said. "Should someone go with you?"

"I will be fine alone," he said. "While I'm gone, you can get to know our companion a little better." He glanced toward Dawnriver.

It might help, she thought. Having time to assess Dawnriver could settle her doubts.

"Then be careful," she said. "I cannot afford to lose you."

Willowvine returned to their assigned rooms, sliding the bag that contained all their research under the couch. The room had been cleared, but the university director assured them they could have access for as long as they wanted.

She placed her own wards on the room after dropping the other bags in a corner. She would leave them packed so her group could make a fast exit.

"I don't feel like sitting in the rooms," Tom said. "Can we find a place outside?"

Willowvine understood his feelings. The room seemed cramped when she expected to be on the road already. She strengthened the wards so that she would be warned if anyone even tried to enter without permission. No one would be able to pass, but knowing that an attempt was made would give her reason to investigate.

"I think there's a courtyard garden near the dining hall," she said. "Perhaps it will be a good place for Dawnriver to give you a lesson. I would love to observe. Healing has always been something I wished I had a talent for." She ushered them out of the room and set the protections.

"An excellent idea," Dawnriver said when they found him. "I have been there, and the garden will give us many opportunities for you both to learn how to use plants when Tom or I are busy."

"Fine, but why would I need to know that?" Tom asked as

they strolled the corridor toward the courtyard. "I can heal people and animals."

"That is why I'm here," Dawnriver said. "There are a number of reasons that a healer would need plant knowledge. Can you think of them?"

Willowvine liked his teaching style. If he told Tom the answer, the boy would have no stake in the knowledge.

"Do any of them enhance my ability?" Tom asked.

"Yes, and another reason?"

Willowvine smiled and kept her urge to answer under control.

Tom thought in silence as they passed into the courtyard. Willowvine asked a server for tea and then settled on one of the stone benches. The courtyard was designed in a hexagram, with raised beds filling most of the area. Paths wound between the beds. The wall containing them was wide enough to use as a seat. If their mission wasn't so vital, Willowvine would have taken advantage of her new-found legitimacy to linger here for days.

"Some things cannot be healed with power? And maybe I can't heal everyone or every animal that way?"

"Good," Dawnriver said. "You will also get tired, and your powers will drain. It is simple in this small group for you to husband your energy. It will be a different matter in the future. I suggest you start your own collection of dried plants and herbs that can be carried with you."

"And if you know the properties of plants, you can ask for help even if there is no other healer around." Willowvine ran her fingers through a low shrub, raising a clean scent.

The tea arrived and along with it, Needleblade. Her disappointment at the intrusion soured the lightness that she'd felt at the quiet.

"I don't think I can imagine a nicer way to spend these hours of delay than with you. Where is Springheart?"

"He is working with the Scree woman to find our horses," Dawnriver said. "I am about to begin a lesson on medicinal plants."

Willowvine knew it was meant to dismiss Needleblade, but he seemed oblivious.

"A subject I know well," Needleblade said. He seated himself next to Willowvine. "I'm happy to assist."

No one had requested his help. Willowvine was tempted to be blunt in asking him to leave, but as she opened her mouth, she changed her mind. This might be a good opportunity to learn more about Needleblade. Perhaps her suspicions were unfounded, or perhaps not. She wouldn't find out without talking to him. It was not possible to use her own powers to read his aura because it required her to enter a light trance. There was no way he would miss that.

"What is this plant used for?" she asked both elves.

"It is wonderful with fowl," Dawnriver said.

"And cleaning wounds if boiled in clean water," Needleblade added. "I thought the point was to teach the boy the medicinal qualities."

"Yes, but I think it important that my students understand the whole picture, not just one side of it," Dawnriver said.

"Then I bow to your expertise," Needleblade said. "I'm sure you have a lot of experience in teaching."

That made Willowvine curious. They only had Zerenia's word that Dawnriver was a teacher. She kept the thought to herself, preferring to let the two elves reveal their characters through their chatter.

"It would be easier for me if only one of you taught," Tom said. He pointed to a leafy plant. "What is this useful for?"

Needleblade nodded to Dawnriver as if to say, 'I'm not interfering'.

"Taking the sting from an insect bite. It will help to heal a shallow wound. You need to chew the leaves before using it to release the sap."

"It tastes awful," Needleblade added. "You will be better off saving your power for that type of healing."

"And you have experience with that?" Dawnriver asked.

"A little, but I am not a healer," Needleblade said.

Listening to them bicker was entertaining. Willowvine sipped her tea and observed as each one vied for the honor of telling Tom the most interesting information on each plant. Her plan to dig deeper into Dawnriver's past, and perhaps find a way to trust him, was not possible without interrupting the flow of verbal sparring and she had no energy to think of a way to do that politely. At least Tom was learning. And Dawnriver was a much better tutor than Needleblade.

SPRINGHEART MADE his way to their rooms, brushing away the dust from his clothes. The only good thing about his search for the horses was the short time he'd been away. He didn't know how to break the news to Tom about the slaughter. An hour's run from the stable the bodies lay in piles, only their horses had been killed.

Whoever took the animals wanted them to know the attack was targeted. There were plenty of hoof prints around the massacre to show the other animals still lived. He expected they were on their way to an auction, ownership markings masked by spells.

He stopped at the door, noticing Willowvine's wards. He could disable them, but it would be better to leave their belongings safe. She couldn't have gone far. He headed to the dining hall, stopping to ask if anyone knew where she was. It turned out she was settled in the adjoining garden. He ordered a meal and went to join her.

She sat on the edge of one of the planters and observed as

Tom talked with Dawnriver and Needleblade about something growing there. He didn't care for Needleblade's presence, but other than being outright rude, he saw no way to dislodge him from their party until they left.

"This looks peaceful," he said as he lowered himself to sit beside Willowvine.

"It's not," she said. "Listen to them."

He turned to watch the three who were still at the same planter bed. After a few moments, he grunted. "Do they think there will be a prize?"

"For teaching Tom the most?" She laughed. "He's doing as much teaching as learning. Neither of them is an expert."

"Did you get a chance to check their auras?"

"No. I can now if you think it's important." She shifted a little so that she was hidden behind Springheart.

He told her about the horses, adding, "Tom will be heartbroken."

"Yes, but it must have been someone in the university. Do you think one of them..." She pointed toward Needleblade and Dawnriver.

"It's possible," he said. "You should check them, now. I don't want to leave here wondering if we're carrying our enemy with us."

He watched as she entered the trance. To anyone it would look like a nap, but he knew she was more aware of the world now than when she was on alert.

"Your meal." The waiter spoke quietly, but it interrupted Willowvine's concentration. She had her hand on her weapon as she opened her eyes.

The waiter pointed to where the food was on a table set in the shade. "I have a message for you." He handed Willowvine a folded paper and then left.

"Did you see anything?" Springheart asked.

"Only that they both hide secrets," she said. "That is true about everyone."

She called the others to the meal. She invited Needleblade to join them. He accepted after a weak refusal. "You really don't have to include me."

"Our pleasure," Willowvine said. She opened the paper the waiter had handed her, read the contents, and slipped it into her pouch.

Springheart tried to think of a way to dig deeper into the secret but couldn't come up with something that was subtle enough to use in public.

"I assume we are all leaving when the horses arrive tomorrow," Needleblade said.

"Everyone will be in a hurry," Springheart said. "It would be better to choose an animal and then wait the rush out."

"And they may not come in the morning," Dawnriver said.

"I'm sure if the horses are delayed, some people will choose to walk to the village." Willowvine looked at Springheart as she spoke. It was an offer of a second plan.

It was a good plan. If they walked, they could leave when they wanted and avoid Needleblade. But as humans didn't travel as quickly as elves, Tom would be at a disadvantage. Springheart nodded, hoping she would think of a way for the boy to keep up.

One of the scholars came to the table. "I'm sorry to interrupt your meal," he said. "We need healers and I understand you have two in your party."

Dawnriver stood, taking a last gulp of tea. "Of course, we will assist."

"I'm afraid assisting is not what we require. Our own healers have fallen sick as well as a number of our scholars. You would be the only ones."

Tom stood. "Then we'd best get started," he said. He turned to Dawnriver. "I guess I'll use the lesson sooner than I expected. We need someone to help us by creating potions and poultices from the garden."

They left and Springheart turned to Needleblade. This would be a good opportunity to question his motives.

"I hope this illness won't inconvenience you," Needleblade said. "Is it possible that your healers will not wish leave sick people to fend for themselves?"

The thought had not occurred to Springheart. "I'm sure arrangements can be made," he said.

Willowvine leaned across to take the last piece of fruit "Someone will go to the village and bring help if this is not easily healed. I hope you will not suffer from the illness, or an inability to continue on your way."

"As long as I can get a horse under me, I'll be fine."

"Where is your next stop?" Springheart asked.

"I head inland, and you?"

"Along the coast," Springheart lied. He knew they could pretend to travel in that direction for long enough to fool someone wishing to follow.

"Then we may not meet again," Needleblade said. "I hope you have a safe journey."

Springheart wished him the same and watched as he walked into the dining hall.

"Walking?" Willowvine said. "I know I suggested it, but won't we take too long?"

"It's just to the village. We could go now," Springheart said. He turned to see the stable master heading their way. "This doesn't look like good news."

"I see you are enjoying your enforced stay," the stable master said. "Thank you for bringing the news, and I assure you we will replace your horses at no cost."

"We appreciate that," Willowvine said. "I think we need to let Tom know soon, since the news is out."

"A tragedy. I know the boy was attached to them," the stable master said. "Unfortunately, I bring more bad news."

Springheart knew the only bad news was that they couldn't leave tomorrow. "When will horses arrive?"

"It will be very late tomorrow. And when they arrive, they will need rest and food."

"So, another day's delay," Springheart said. "We must have the first choice of the replacements, and our healer will check them out before we accept them."

"Of course," the stable master said.

"Walking is sounding more attractive," Willowvine said. "Now to tell Tom the bad news and try to convince our healers that they must leave their patients when we are ready."

Springheart rose. "The message? Was it from Leafcreek? Will he be able to replace the letters he gave us?"

"It's from Lakewing," she said. "Leafcreek is failing. They don't want to disturb him unless it's vital."

"We can manage," Springheart said. "We've accomplished more on less than what we have now."

"I hope so," she said.

Chapter 17

She'd convinced Springheart to stay in their rooms while she sought out Tom. Not that the news would be better coming from her, she just couldn't sit still, and their belongings needed a guard.

Walking the halls looking for them, she realized how many of the university residents were ill. It hadn't affected any of the visitors as far as she knew. Asking people she met in the halls led her from one sick room to another, just missing the healers each time. It seemed like half the scholars suffered with this disease.

She couldn't keep following behind them and never catching up. If she didn't find them soon, Tom would hear the news before she could get to him.

She reached Stonerose's room to find he'd also succumbed. To be ill twice in such a short time was the worst kind of luck. He'd only had the chance to point them in the right direction for clues and then been too sick to help further. She stood at his door intending to ask about Tom and Dawnriver. "Is this the same illness?"

"It seems so," Stonerose said, his voice wheezing. "I think I may be the source, that I brought the sickness here."

"Have you seen Tom?"

"The healers came a while ago," he said. "I dozed, so it's hard to say how much time has passed. They are working together. A student came with medicine after they left."

"Did they say how long you would be ill?"

"They are kind and encouraging. If we survive the initial bout and receive care, we should begin to mend in a few days."

"So, they know what it is?"

"No," Stonerose said. "But please don't spread that. I think they want people feeling optimistic."

His eyes drooped and Willowvine said goodbye. If Dawnriver didn't know what this illness was, how would she persuade him and Tom to leave? It saddened her to think only she and Springheart would be continuing their quest.

A student in blue robes rushed past Willowvine. "Wait," she called to the girl. "Have you seen the healers?"

The student pointed down a side corridor and kept moving.

As she entered the corridor, Willowvine heard Dawnriver's voice. "Sleep is your best cure."

She slipped into the chamber to see Tom place his hands on the scholar's chest and close his eyes to pour healing power into the patient; a goblin whose skin was almost gray with the sickness.

"Don't come closer," Dawnriver said. "We have taken precautions, but I don't want you contracting this disease."

"I need to speak with Tom," she said. "It will only take a moment." Her news would hurt for longer than that.

"This is the last new patient," Dawnriver said. "Tom will need rest before we start checking on the progress of the others."

Willowvine slipped back into the hallway to wait and think.

Unlike the horses, this illness couldn't be an attack on them. It must be just an awful coincidence that they were here when it happened. None of her party were falling ill. If it was aimed at them, surely the most effective way to delay their journey would be to cause them to be ill, not these scholars.

Tom and Dawnriver joined her a moment later.

"What did you want me for?" Tom asked.

She saw the lines of fatigue around his eyes. That made it harder to speak. "I'm sorry, Tom. Springheart is back and the horses...our horses are dead."

"The others?" Tom asked, his voice catching.

"Still alive when Springheart turned back."

Tom rubbed his face and looked at Dawnriver. "I think I'm too tired to take it in," he said. "Someone stole our horses, all the horses, just to kill them? To keep us here, right?"

"And now this illness," Dawnriver said.

"You think this was done by someone?" Willowvine asked. "Not a natural disease?"

Tom started walking away. "We shouldn't talk here," he said.

Willowvine noticed him wipe his eyes as they walked. He led them to the kitchen where he asked for wine and food. "I'm falling asleep as I talk to my patients," he said. "I hope food will help me to go on a bit longer."

"You should rest," Willowvine said. "Both of you."

"We will," Dawnriver said. "But talk first. This illness is a problem. We don't know what it is. The patients are responding well, but I'm worried that Stonerose recovered from the first bout and then succumbed again."

Food arrived, and Tom poured wine. "We'll have more information in a few hours," he said. "If the healers recover, there is hope, but I can't leave until we know the sick are taken care of."

He sounded so final. Tom wasn't offering, he was telling

her the way it would be. She had no idea that with training Tom would become so confident; he hardly sounded like a boy any more. "If it comes to that, we'll see."

Dawnriver swirled the wine in his glass. "You should not continue alone," he said. "This is too important to risk you and Springheart. Now that the patients are under care, they won't need two of us. I'll stay."

That relieved some of Willowvine's worry. She felt the need to have Tom with them. As if something was directing her actions and wanted her to have these companions. Or perhaps because she cared for the boy and didn't want to leave him here. As for Dawnriver, if he offered to stay, he couldn't be conspiring against them, could he?

"Perhaps a healer could come from the village?" Willowvine suggested.

"Someone went to ask," Tom said. "If we can figure out what the illness is, it will help."

"How much time do you need?" Willowvine asked. If it was a matter of a day, they could wait.

"Rest and then we'll have more information on how our efforts worked." Dawnriver yawned. "Let's get back to the rooms before we must be carried there."

"Do you think it was quick?" Tom asked as they walked back.

"The horses?" Willowvine asked. "I think so, but you will have to ask Springheart for details."

THE DAY HAD CRAWLED BY. Willowvine agonized over how to move forward. If the illness was contagious, would they be quarantined? How long would that delay them? Would someone get to the Stone first? If they left now, and quarantine was declared, would they be spreading this illness as they passed? If they did that, the rest of the elves would have a reason to blame and shun orphans regardless of what happened with the Stone. Would the healers even let them leave?

It was late, and the others were sleeping. They'd piled into the one room rather than to their separate ones. It felt safer and easier to run if they needed to leave. But the closeness stifled her. She couldn't sleep. Every time she tried, images of slaughtered horses filled her mind only to be replaced with a dream of the Stones of Power slipping away from her.

She looked around and noticed that Dawnriver had not returned from his trip to check on the patients earlier. Tom lay curled in his blanket, deeply asleep. She slipped into the hallway, closing the door behind her gently. It made her shoulders twitch to leave her wards deactivated, but the healers refused to stay unless they could be reached by anyone in need.

The halls were quiet except for the occasional moan or coughing fit from someone fighting the effects of the illness. The high arches of the ceiling and the long, uninterrupted line of sight helped her feel peace. She didn't want to disturb anyone, so running the halls was out of the question, even though burning off the frustration would be easier at a full run. She settled for a quick pace leading toward the archives.

She might as well continue reading anything she could find as long as she was stuck at the university. Their destination was the Library at the Center, so perhaps a little more research on that building would help.

The path to the archives took her past most of the guest quarters. The sounds of illness faded, replaced by some magnificent snoring, and some quiet conversations. She felt like they were missing something about the situation. A disease was usually not so discriminating. She could only hope that it was something the scholars and students were exposed to that visitors hadn't caused.

A door opened ahead of her. Dawnriver slipped through

and carefully closed it before turning. He started at the sight of her. She watched him take control of himself before he took a step toward her.

"That's Needleblade's room," she said.

"It is," Dawnriver said. "I was checking on him."

She could see the lie written on the way he wouldn't look at her. "Is the disease spreading?"

"No." He looked over her shoulder and then behind them. "We should talk."

"Yes." She closed the distance between them. "What have you done?"

Chapter 18

They found an alcove halfway down the corridor. It was large enough to hide them from casual view, and there were no chamber doors nearby to hide eavesdroppers.

"What did you do?" she asked again. This time she was going to get answers.

"I didn't do anything. I was searching for something I thought Needleblade had."

"What made you think there was anything to find?"

"Don't pretend you trust him — or me," Dawnriver said. "I don't blame you. It's not like anything up to now has set you up to trust strangers. I thought having Zerenia introduce us might be enough, but...it doesn't matter right now."

"You need to start explaining," she said. "I will happily have you detained if I don't hear a good reason for you being in his room. You say Zerenia recommended you, but we have no confirmation of it. When we left the Guardian, we were expecting someone else to send a tutor for Tom."

"I was hoping to be wrong," Dawnriver said. "This illness is similar to the symptoms of baneroot poisoning."

"I thought it was like something else," she said. "Tom is convinced it's a disease."

"I didn't want him to know," Dawnriver said. "After hearing about his horses, I didn't want to burden him with this."

"Stop protecting him," Willowvine said. "He won't thank you, and he's much tougher than you think."

"I'll take your word for it." He looked into her eyes, as if assessing her. Then after a deep breath, he said, "It's because we're not sick that I suspected poison. I haven't trusted how Needleblade joined us. I tried to talk to him, but he is evasive when we touch on personal topics."

"I've found the same with both of you," Willowvine said.

"I decided to search his room. I thought it would set my mind at ease. I'm a healer. I want to stop this illness and I need the cause to do that. There is no other reason."

"And?"

"I found it, baneroot, in his pack."

"Where is he?"

"Studying in the archives."

"Is there another reason someone would carry baneroot?"

"No, but to be honest, he could be transporting it for someone."

At least my suspicions weren't completely off target. "I don't think that's likely. He was supposed to be coming here to teach. Why would he bring poison? We need him to answer to it."

She turned to run toward the archives.

"No." Dawnriver held out his hand. "We are at an advantage now. He doesn't know I found it."

"You left it with him? Was that smart if you think he's poisoning people?"

"If he thinks he's gotten away with it, we can use that against him," Dawnriver said. "If it is baneroot poisoning, we can cure these people in a few hours. Then we can go."

"Assuming I want a sneak like you with us." Willowvine wanted to simply confront Needleblade, to get the truth and be done. She knew it wouldn't be easy, but it would put an end to the suspicions. Politeness had no place in these situations.

"You need me," he said.

"Why?"

He looked at her again and she could see he struggled with something by the way his eyes narrowed, and his lips twitched as though he was fighting the urge to speak.

"I'm not what you were led to believe," he said, finally.

"That isn't a surprise," Willowvine said. She braced herself for an attack, hand on knife, muscles ready to spring.

"We hoped it could be a secret much longer than this. But I was sent from Treepond as an agent of her faction."

Willowvine relaxed a little, still not ready to trust, but having Leafcreek's friend as a reference helped ease her fears. "Faction? You mean another secret group?"

He nodded. "I'm not sure how secret we have been, but yes, we are not official. How much do you know about the Council of Elves?"

She hadn't had much contact with them outside her quests. For Willowvine, the council represented everything that kept her from being part of Elven society. "Assume I know nothing," she said.

"The council is not always in full agreement about policy," he said. "There are two factions debating at the moment. Both with their supporters, what you might call spies."

"Is this something the others should hear?" If he intended her to keep this from Springheart, he would be wrong. "Tom is relying on you to teach him."

Dawnriver glanced around the empty hallway. "It would be better to keep this between us. All my training says the more people you bring into a secret, the higher the risk it will no longer remain one. My true mission is a weapon we can use."

He looked at her for long enough that Willowvine became uncomfortable. Then he sighed and said, "No, I see that's a step too far. You can pass on anything I tell you, but I need to speak to the university leaders as soon as we are done here."

"Okay," she said, leaning against the wall with her arms crossed. "I'm listening."

He paused again, looking at his hands and collecting his thoughts. "I'm not prepared with a lesson, so there may be gaps in what I tell you. I will be happy to fill in the details when we are on the road."

"I won't ask a question unless I need clarification right now." She understood the impatience. The longer they stood here the more likely they would be interrupted, and if what Dawnriver had found about the poison was true, it couldn't wait.

"Treepond is the head of the faction that believes the Stones of Power should be returned, and exiling orphans is needlessly cruel. One of the reasons she's so close to Leafcreek is to stay aware of the developments. The fact they are friends is a bonus."

"I thought you didn't have time to lecture?"

"Yes. The other faction, I'm sure you've guessed, wants things to stay as they are. All of this is in the open and dressed up as policy debate, but it's not intellectual disagreement. Behind each faction are the believers. People like Waterfeather. They will do anything to keep the Stones apart."

Willowvine nodded. She'd had a taste of that fanaticism.

"Someone directed him," Dawnriver said. "We don't know who, but they won't give up. I'm here to help protect you so the Orphan Stone can be restored to the maze."

"A believer?" Willowvine asked. She didn't care what side he was on, if he was a fanatic, they would part ways.

"Not in that sense. Like Treepond, I believe the world will be better if the Stones are returned to the maze, and I never agreed with the policy for orphans. But there are lines I can't cross without facing repercussions and still keep my identity secret. You see why I couldn't tell you?"

Chapter 19

"Why should I believe you?" Willowvine asked.

She hadn't used her powers on him with any depth, but perhaps she should now, when there wouldn't be an interruption. She wanted to trust him. He would be a good ally if he was telling the truth. If he wasn't, would she read it in his aura, or could he mask what she saw?

"My sincere words didn't convince you?" He smiled. "I anticipated it coming to this before I joined you." He reached into the neck of his tunic and drew out a crystal on a chain. "Treepond will respond if we call her."

Willowvine wished she wasn't alone with him. If she could talk to Treepond while reading Dawnriver's aura it would be perfect. But in the trance, she wouldn't hear anything else and there was no one to take the other part. "Call her."

While he whispered some words over the crystal, Willowvine tried to read him a little deeper than in the garden. A glance at his aura made her more confident in his story. There was no shadow that would indicate a hidden intent. A light read didn't allay all her fears, but she would make the opportunity to read deeper before they left the university.

"Willowvine." Treepond's voice preceded her image.

"Do you know why we called you?" Willowvine asked as a mirage of the other elf rose from the crystal.

"I assume you uncovered Dawnriver's true purpose."

"Is he really your agent?"

"Yes. I argued for full disclosure at the outset, but was persuaded secrecy might draw out the agents of our mysterious enemy."

"Is he a healer?" Willowvine grinned at Dawnriver. "Tom seems more experienced than him. I'm surprised we didn't catch him out sooner."

Treepond laughed. "I would not have sent him if he couldn't offer value. But I admit his healing knowledge is more academic than practical. Perhaps now his identity is in the open, he can be of more help. I think it would be safer if you kept his secret from others."

"Not from Springheart and Tom. I won't keep secrets from them," she said. "Do you think someone is after us? The attack at the camp, the horses, the sickness, are they all directed at our mission?"

"I've reported the incidents," Dawnriver said. "All except what I just learned." He told Treepond about the poison.

"I will investigate this Needleblade," she said. "Is there any proof other than the poison that he has bad intent?"

"My instinct isn't sufficient?" Dawnriver asked.

"I also feel he is not to be trusted," Willowvine said. "But that's not enough either."

"Then I think you avoid him and leave it to me." Treepond looked over her shoulder and back. "I must leave you. Willowvine, I hope you can take my word that Dawnriver is your ally." The image faded away.

Dawnriver slid the crystal back inside his tunic. "I must go, too. If we are to administer the antidote to the poison as a test, it must be done soon."

"Should we be worried about being poisoned?"

"I think the attack is confined to the scholars. Perhaps it was an experiment and he'll try for you next. Take care what you eat and drink."

"Come back to the rooms when you're finished," Willowvine said. "I'll tell Springheart and Tom about this."

"If you are determined to reveal my secret, then let me be the one to explain," he said. "I can answer their questions. And if you still doubt me, you can read my aura." He left without looking back.

He knows what I can do? That was supposed to be secret.

SPRINGHEART HELD the door open so Willowvine could slip through to the courtyard. They were leaving the university in the middle of the night before someone could poison them. He'd been skeptical when Willowvine first told them about the illness, but when Dawnriver returned an hour later and confirmed the patients were responding to the antidote, Springheart insisted they pack and leave. No one resisted the idea.

"We can pick up food at the village," Willowvine said. "I'm not eating or drinking anything else from here."

So, here they were a few hours before dawn, creeping out a side door like thieves. Or like they'd done numerous times when they were couriers.

Willowvine signaled the front court was clear. Springheart sent Tom out, then Dawnriver, and finally followed, closing the door silently.

The university was surrounded by a wide courtyard and a gated wall. The wall protected the three main buildings, and the gate was closed after dinner and opened before breakfast. It was never completely locked. He watched as each of his companions ran to the gate and slipped into the shadows at the side. Tom moved as lightly as an elf, and as fast, but he would tire much quicker. The village was hours away at human pace, but they would be on horses by midday.

Springheart joined them at the gate. "That group of trees," he said, pointing east. "We wait there. From that point we can travel together. No one will hear us."

Once again, Willowvine led the way. It took her only moments to reach the trees. She leaped to the lower branch to watch for any danger. Their fears that someone at the university would attack wasn't the only concern. It would have been bandits who took the horses, no matter who ordered them to do it. If they were getting bolder, more caution was needed.

Tom and Dawnriver went together across the open field to the haven of the trees. When they were within the shadows, Springheart checked the gate was firmly closed and then ran to join them.

"How are you doing, Tom?" Dawnriver asked.

"As long as we don't have too many runs like that, I'll be fine." He adjusted the straps of the bags he carried. "I'll try not to slow you down too much."

"Don't be a hero, yet," Willowvine said as she dropped to the ground beside them. "We don't have to rush to the village. We need you strong enough to check the horses when we get there."

"Are you headed to the village, too?" Needleblade joined them under the tree. He'd run across while they'd talked to Tom.

Springheart cursed his inattention. "I thought you were staying until the horses arrived."

"I became afraid I would contract that disease and be confined there until I recovered or died."

Chapter 20

Willowvine knew he lied. Even without using her powers, knowing Dawnriver found the poison in his room confirmed everything she feared. And now, just when people might start asking questions, he was fleeing. She was tempted to ask him outright.

"I hear they are all on the mend," she said. "You don't need to put up with the walk. I'm sure the horses will arrive today, and you can be on your way in relative comfort."

Needleblade looked back at the building as if he was considering her advice. He sighed and turned to her. "Like you, I think going to the village is a better option. Who knows what else might happen to delay me if I stay."

Why couldn't he leave them alone? Willowvine looked at her companions, hoping one of them would give an answer. No one spoke.

"Please don't allow us to slow you down," she said with a nod to Tom.

"I do feel the need of a rest," Tom said.

"I think that the safety companions bring on a dark road is more valuable than speed today." Needleblade dug into one of his bags. "I have a potion here that might help restore your energy, Tom."

"That's not necessary," Dawnriver said, stepping between them. "I can heal the boy if he needs it."

"Then perhaps we should be on our way," Needleblade said. "The sooner we start, the sooner we will be at our destination."

He's not going to leave us.

Willowvine gave up on trying to separate Needleblade from their party. Their roads diverged at the village, and Needleblade would find it harder sticking to them when he'd already said he was heading inland.

"We'll keep to the road," she said. "Keep your ears open for riders. If we are attacked, don't get in our way."

She ran down the slope to the road and stood there, hands on hips, waiting.

THE MAIN ROAD turned out to wind its way through the countryside, making the journey slower than Willowvine hoped. Tom kept up because he wasn't having to climb over the small hills surrounding them, but it felt to Willowvine like they should have arrived by now, that they had walked the distance to the village twice.

"Should we leave the road?" Dawnriver asked. "We'll get to the village past noon if we can only go this fast."

Willowvine glanced around her. The road wandered between a thin line of trees set to break the wind. Behind those was a rocky terrain of hills and valleys. "Do you think we can find a more direct route?"

"There's a reason the road winds," Needleblade said. "We should trust the elves who designed the route."

Willowvine had been watching him for signs that he was the one who poisoned the scholars. He'd walked with them without complaint but had talked the entire way. If they had need for stealth, would he be able to suppress his chatter?

"Things may have changed since then," she said. "The three of us only traveled this road on horses before. Let me check to see if we can leave the road safely."

She ran through the screen of trees and scrambled up the side of the hill. Stones flew from under her feet, and she reached the top scratched and out of breath. The trip down was easier only because she lost her footing and slid to the bottom.

She slipped back through the trees, brushing the dirt from her scratches. "We'll stick to the road."

Dawnriver and Tom took her hands and poured healing energy into her body. The rush of power made her light-headed, but when they were done, there was no sign of any injury.

"What's that?" Needleblade asked.

The sound of hoofbeats came closer. Then a jangle of armor and the clank of sword sheaths hitting metal. Travelers from the village ahead.

Willowvine signaled them to get through the trees and hide, running behind with her bow drawn in case they didn't make it.

The party passed without noticing them. Willowvine knew it was only because the sun hadn't risen, and darkness provided concealment. The trees didn't give much cover.

"I'M SORRY," Tom said. "I need a rest. How much farther is it, do you think?"

"We will be there soon," Needleblade said. "I seem to remember this view. I passed this way before, but not on foot. Perhaps another hour?"

Willowvine wondered why Needleblade kept that to

himself. He could have said that it would take more than a couple of hours on foot and the surroundings were too rough to use as an alternative. It was one more little cut at his reputation; he could not be trusted. Perhaps he wasn't an agent of the same organization that Waterfeather had been, but it did not make him their friend.

"There's a clearing ahead," she said. "Just before the next turn."

The thought of a rest added speed to their steps. Within minutes, they stood on the soft grass beside a well that held cool, sweet water.

Tom put his bags on the ground and lay down. "I'm happy we'll have horses soon," he said. "You would be forced to leave me behind to walk to our destination."

"Is it a long way?" Needleblade asked.

Willowvine held her breath. Was Tom so tired he would slip up and say where they were going?

"If it's more than ten steps," Tom said. "It's a long distance at this point."

Willowvine chuckled with the others. "It's more than that to the village," she said.

An arrow sank into the ground at her feet.

"Stay down," she said, hearing an echo in Springheart's yell.

She pulled her bow into place and set an arrow, searching for a target. No other arrows flew toward them.

"Come out," Springheart called.

Willowvine concentrated on finding the attacker. She heard knives being drawn. Tom, Dawnriver, and Needleblade all prepared for a close-in fight.

A twig snapped behind her. Willowvine spun and let her arrow fly. Two bandits crept up from the rear. Only one continued.

She missed with the second arrow.

"You are outnumbered and surrounded," a voice said from the cover of an alder. "Just give us your valuables and we might not kill you."

"Show yourselves and we might let you live," Springheart said.

"We are too hungry to let you defeat us," the voice said.

Willowvine made sure Needleblade and Dawnriver were placed to attack the bandit who still approached and then scanned the area with her powers. The moment's inattention because of the trance would not add to the danger; knowing how many attackers waited would reduce it.

"There are five of them," she said. "You do not outnumber us. One of yours is dead."

"He was not my favorite," the bandit said, his anger at her discovery evident in the pinched quality of the words.

"If you withdraw now," Springheart said, "we won't pursue."

Willowvine wished again she didn't need to drop into a trance to use her powers. Shooting to where the auras had been was a waste of arrows. The speaker hid behind a tree, so she had no clear target.

The only bandit in sight was the one holding a battered sword waiting for orders. She couldn't bring herself to kill him while he stood. She'd been close to this life before and knew the desperation that drove them.

"Are you going to wait all day?" Needleblade asked. "Either leave us or engage. We have places to be."

The arrogant idiot. While she dug for anything that would allow them to walk away, he was provoking. For a second, she wondered if he was doing more than that. Was he ordering his mercenary to attack?

In answer to Needleblade's challenge, another arrow hit one of their packs, just missing Tom. Whoever was shooting was getting more accurate.

Then things moved fast. Three more bandits joined the speaker and rushed their group. Willowvine shot her arrow then dropped the bow in favor of her throwing knives.

Springheart drew his sword as his own bow fell to the ground.

Two of the bandits rushed Needleblade and Dawnriver, who were protecting Tom; two came at Willowvine and Springheart.

She flung her knife, catching one bandit in the throat and ran to Tom's side. She heard a grunt of pain and then Springheart joined them. "It's almost too easy," he said.

"I don't need protecting," Tom said. He held up his own knife.

Willowvine watched the fight between the bandits and the two elves. It was clear neither of her companions were trained to fight, but Dawnriver managed to deflect his attacker while Needleblade's efforts seemed more clumsy luck than fighting skill.

"They need help," Tom said.

"No," Willowvine said, placing her hand on his arm. "We need to wait for an opening."

She looked to Springheart to tell him she'd move in. He was armed with his bow again.

"I just need a clear shot," he said.

Willowvine turned back to the action. "DROP." She felt the rasp in her throat as she gave as much volume to the word as possible.

Dawnriver fell to the ground.

Springheart's arrow lodged in the attacker's heart.

Needleblade still tussled with his bandit.

Springheart could have killed him too, if Needleblade hadn't been so stupid.

Willowvine rushed forward, bending to take Needleblade at

the knees so he would topple. She felt wind whip past her as Springheart shot the last bandit.

The man on the ground still breathed.

She untangled herself from Needleblade and crawled to the dying man's side.

"Not enough money," he wheezed.

"Who paid you?" she asked, fighting the temptation to shake him.

"Is he still talking?" Needleblade asked, drowning out the final words.

Why can't he keep silent?

"He was," she said. "But now he is dead."

She stood to say they should go before the final bandit decided to attack. A ripple of laughter floated across the clearing.

"This is more interesting than simply stealing," Cornflower said.

Willowvine closed her eyes and scanned for the aura. It was already too far away to bother chasing.

Chapter 21

When they made sure the rest of the bandits were dead, Willowvine hurried the company from the clearing. The boost of adrenaline from the fight would carry them farther than a rest. She trailed Needleblade, watching for signs he'd tried to stop the bandit identifying him.

There hadn't been time for discussion on the road, so she couldn't share her suspicions. Everyone kept their reactions quiet as they hurried to the village.

When they arrived, Springheart went to report the incident. Willowvine and the others went to the stables. Needleblade was still with them despite her suggestions he find a place to rest. Tom offered to choose him a horse so he could be on his way.

"Will you be leaving immediately?" she asked Needleblade.

"I have time for a meal," he said. "Please join me. I would pay you for saving my life."

"You've not fought bandits before?" she asked, keeping her gaze on Tom and Dawnriver.

"No. It is different from the classes I took," Needleblade

said. "Did you see how dirty their weapons were? We could have been poisoned by a scratch."

"There's a lot of poisoning and illness going around." Willowvine turned to him.

"Yes," he said. "I'm glad we left that behind."

She wanted him gone now, tired of being polite and having him ignore the hints. "We will be here, making arrangements," she said. "Perhaps it would be better to say our goodbyes now."

"Surely you don't plan to leave right away," Needleblade said. "A little time to recover from the attack?"

"I don't know when we will leave," she said. "But you should say your goodbyes now."

Something hard glittered behind his eyes. Then he smiled and gave a small bow. "Yes, that is probably best. I wish you a safe and pleasant journey."

She nodded and walked to where Tom was selecting their horses. "Tom, do you have a recommendation for Needleblade's horse?"

"That one," he said, nodding to a piebald gelding. "Sturdy and gentle. You'll be happy."

Willowvine stood aside as Needleblade said goodbye to Dawnriver and Tom. Then they were alone with the groom and stable master.

"We will need horses," Willowvine said.

"I've promised them to the university. They'll be on the road in an hour," the stable master said. "That elf took the last horse I had."

"We've come from there," she said. "Our horses were taken." She didn't add the slaughter; another secret to hold tight.

"If that is true, you'll have papers," the stable master held out his hand.

"No. We had to leave in a hurry." She clutched the pouch

containing their last few coins. It didn't feel heavy enough to bribe him, but she had to try. The Library at the Center was too far to walk in the little time they had.

"No point in trying to give me coins," the stable master said. "I do business with the university and you're just passing through. That pouch doesn't hold enough to make it worth messing with my future."

"Willowvine, let's go," Springheart said. "We can't waste time here."

"We need horses," she said. "What if we needed fewer than you are sending to replace ours? Five were stolen, but two will work."

The stable master shook his head and then looked over her shoulder. "Where are you going, Jacob?"

Willowvine turned to see a young goblin running toward the town square.

"Back in a minute." He kept running.

"What about a trade?" Tom asked. He'd stepped between them while Willowvine was distracted. "Some of these horses need healing. I can do that in exchange for you letting us take two."

"They've been looked at, boy," the stable master said. "Our healer found nothing serious wrong."

"Your healer has a different meaning for serious," Tom said.

"They'll be the university's problem if something does go wrong."

"So, you are willing to endanger your relationship with them," Willowvine said. "We just need to find the right price."

"I said no." He walked away.

Springheart picked up her bags. "We have enough to find some lodging," he said. "Perhaps we can negotiate with a private owner."

Willowvine held out her hand for the bags. "Perhaps, if we

left everything but the essentials behind." She glanced over at Tom. "You and I could make it."

"Only if we can't find another way," he said. "If we get attacked again, we need a healer."

"Dawnriver could come," she said. Why was he being so stubborn? Tom would understand, and the Stone was too important.

"Later," he said. "There must be some other horses in the village."

They passed through the door into the village square, which was crowded with the weekly market. Dawnriver and Tom stayed to heal the horses, neither able to walk away from the injuries.

An elf stepped from beside a stall. "Excuse my rudeness, but are you Willowvine?"

"Yes," she said, bracing herself to be told to leave the village.

"I am Bloodroot," he said. "You met my niece in the City?"

How had she managed to offend someone in the City?

"Elderroot? She sent a message to the family about meeting you," Bloodroot prompted.

"The pregnant elf?" Willowvine wondered how the name had slipped her mind.

"Yes. I understand you are having difficulties with the stable master?"

"We need horses," Springheart said.

"He's a good man with a limited view of the world. Let's see what I can do to help." Bloodroot strode into the stable.

Ten minutes later, after money and assurances had been offered, five horses were pulled from the university-bound herd and set aside for them.

Bloodroot passed a coin to the goblin who brought him to the stable and wished them luck on their journey.

"How soon can we go, Tom?" Willowvine asked.

"The horses are ready," he said. "I can load the packs and we can go in about five minutes."

"We need food and rest," she said. If they left now, everyone would see which direction they went. As much as she hated yet another delay, they would be safer leaving in the dark.

Turning to the stable master, she said, "We need someone to watch our belongings until dawn."

"My son will do that," he said, more welcoming now that his purse was full. "Your companion headed to Margaret's inn. I'm sure she will have rooms for all of you."

"Is there another inn?" Willowvine wanted to be as far away as she could be from Needleblade.

"Jarald's place is in the opposite direction," the stable master said. "I guess you don't want that talked about?"

"Your discretion is appreciated," she said.

Springheart handed over the fee for the boy to watch the horses. It left them with nothing. Dawnriver would pay for their lodging, one room to save money.

They followed the directions to the inn, leaving Tom at the stable to do some more healing before he would join them.

"The attack," Springheart said. "I don't know if Tom needs someone to talk with. It was violent and sudden."

"I can talk to him," Dawnriver said. "Is it the first time he's seen violence?"

"No," Springheart said. "But that's two attacks in a short time."

Willowvine couldn't hold it in any longer. "Two attacks that I think were arranged for us. If you count the poisoning at the university, and the theft of our horses, remember they only killed ours, it's too many to be coincidence."

"You think Needleblade had something to do with it," Springheart said.

"I think we should stay away from him," she said. "When

we are on our way, we might be safer than we've been this entire time."

RAINBLOSSOM EXCUSED herself from the small group of people she was pretending to listen to. Supporting her public identity as a hostess and mediator was wearing. When they were sure the Stones would not surface, then she could drop these inane social functions and become the leader of a strong Elven society.

Now, the tug of a spell from her agent allowed her to retreat to a quiet room. Inside, she placed a ward on the door. No one would surprise her, no one would probably even care to come looking.

"What do you have for me?" she asked.

"We are in the village," Needleblade said. "The bandit attack didn't delay us long. In fact, it seems to have made them more determined to leave in secret."

This agent had outlived his usefulness. "Where are they going?"

"I haven't been able to learn that. I lost track of them after we finished at the stables."

"You are an expert at not getting the information I need," she said. "Are you sure you believe in our cause?"

"More than ever," he said hurriedly. "The orphans have too much confidence. They need to face the truth."

The truth as her faction defined it, Rainblossom thought. "Do you suspect they already left?"

"They booked a room at another inn," he said. "I can track them down and try again."

"No," Rainblossom said as she put a new plan together in her mind. "Spy, but do not contact. You are to find out when they plan to leave without speaking to any of their party."

"Should I follow them when they go?"

"Just find out when."

She heard faint words of agreement as she severed the connection.

TOM RUBBED the legs of the pack horse. "We're going on an adventure," he murmured to the animal. "I'll take care of you, don't worry. I won't let you or your friends out of my sight. No one will steal you or kill you. I've learned to take more care."

He'd told Willowvine he would stay at the stable, that they should just come when they were ready. It wouldn't be long now; a few hours and they'd be on the next leg of the quest. He felt excitement every time that thought intruded, then a wave of sadness. Would he go back to Sir Jode's stable afterward? He missed his family, even if they weren't related by blood. But he wanted the freedom to wander. Willowvine no longer seemed to suspect Dawnriver; perhaps he had proved to be a real ally. They could travel together. It would give them something to talk about on the road. Maybe he could get Dawnriver to open up about his past. Willowvine might be convinced that he was a friend, but Tom wasn't sure his feelings went that deep.

He gave a final pat to the pack horse and headed for the corner where the stable boys rested, looking for a bite of food and some water.

"My friends. Do you remember them?"

It was Needleblade. He was standing close to a stable boy who was oiling some tack.

Tom took a step into the shadows of an empty stall.

"I don't talk about customers," the boy said.

"Admirable," Needleblade said. "I wanted to give them a token of mine, to bring them luck on their journey."

"Sounds like a nice thing to do," the boy said. He put down

the leather straps and picked up a metal bit. Switching rags, he started to polish it.

"I don't want to miss them," Needleblade said. "They are eager and rise much earlier than I do. Perhaps if I miss them here, I could catch up with them on the road?"

"Maybe." The boy shifted his grip on the bit.

From his position, Tom could see that the stable boy was ready to defend himself. Needleblade was oblivious.

"Do you know which road they're taking?"

"Customers don't tell us where they're going usually."

If Needleblade hoped to learn their destination, he was out of luck. Not only was the boy unwilling to talk, he didn't know.

"You don't know where they intend to take your livestock?"

"Not if they buy them," the boy said, hefting the metal in his hand.

Tom looked at Needleblade but there was no reaction to the implied threat.

"Do you know when they intend to leave?" Needleblade asked the question as he dropped a handful of twigs at the boy's feet.

It was a truth spell. Tom could feel its effects as a slight nudge to step forward. The spell didn't discriminate against the type of deception. The boy would be defenseless against it.

"Midnight," he said.

"And where?"

"I don't know."

Tom held tightly to the open gate of the stall. The stable boy knew he was there. If Needleblade asked the right question it would be all over.

"I suppose I believe you," Needleblade said. He reached for the bit and removed it from the boy's hand. "You won't need this." In one swift move, he collected the twigs from the ground and hit the stable boy on the side of his head.

"That will give you an excuse," he said, then turned to march away.

As soon as it was safe, Tom ran to the boy. He touched the wound and healed the damage. He woke the boy and told him to watch the stables.

"That elf?"

"Not a good one," Tom said. "I'll be back soon." He ran to the inn to find his friends.

Chapter 22

"We must leave now," Willowvine said when Tom reported.

"I have to get back," he said. "I'm afraid of what Needle-blade might do to stop us."

"If we had time, I would stop him," Springheart said. "But I think it's safer for us to be long gone by the time he comes looking."

"Is the stable boy hurt badly?" Dawnriver asked. "I can come with you and help heal him."

"I did it before I came," Tom said, then ran from the room.

Willowvine checked the bags they'd brought with them; a few items were strewn about the room. "Hurry. We can't chance him having a spy here." She stuffed the loose things into the bags.

Springheart rushed them through the door. "I'll settle our bill and be right behind you."

"Someone should make sure Needleblade isn't hanging around the stable," Dawnriver said, tossing Springheart his purse.

Every detail delayed them precious seconds. "Let's get our

bags there first," she said. "I can use my powers to see if I can find his aura."

They ran down the stairs, making no sound as only elves could. Springheart went to wake the innkeeper. Willowvine and Dawnriver hurried to the stable.

Tom had three of the horses saddled and ready to go. He held out his hands for the remaining bags and tied them to the pack animal.

Willowvine pulled the tack from a hook on the wall and began preparing the final horse.

"Can you scan and do that at the same time?" Dawnriver asked.

"No." She looked at the horse and shook her head. "Just check the area quickly."

He ran from the stable.

"Do you think we're safe?" Tom asked. "And the people here. I'd hate to find out they were punished by Needleblade."

"We can't help them," Willowvine said. She grunted as she lifted the saddle onto the horse. "Or no more than leaving them behind. They will be fine." She wished she believed that.

"Give me a minute," Tom said. He rushed to the back of the stable.

Willowvine heard hushed voices, then Tom ran back. He checked that she'd tightened the straps properly.

"I told them to be ready," he said. "One of them went to get the stable master."

"Good." Willowvine looked toward the door. Where are Dawnriver and Springheart?

A shadow slipped in as if in answer to her question. She gripped the haft of a throwing knife in case.

"No one is nearby," Dawnriver said as he stepped into the light.

"I told the innkeeper we were headed south," Springheart said. "It should misdirect Needleblade, give us a head start."

"Do we know where his inn is?" Tom asked as they all mounted. He took the pack animal's lead and nudged his own horse forward.

"No." Willowvine regretted not finding out. "We should go as silently as we can until we're clear of the village."

She urged her horse forward and led them from the stable at a walk.

"WILL THE BOY REMEMBER YOU?" Rainblossom asked. She only cared if he could interfere.

"Between the spell and the head injury, he won't remember what happened."

"Now we just need to know which road." Rainblossom looked at a map of the area surrounding Needleblade's location. It was unfortunate that more than one road crossed the village.

"I will watch as they leave. We will have a direction soon after midnight," Needleblade said. "I can follow at a distance."

"No." Rainblossom was tired of being removed from the action. Needleblade was erratic in his behavior and had only found one decent piece of information. "Just report which road they take. Someone else will take over. You have been compromised." Cornflower would do a much better job than Needleblade.

"The direction they take at first might be a ruse," Needleblade said. "I really should follow for a while to ensure they don't turn off."

"I said no." Rainblossom glared at him, but it was only for show. She had already dismissed him in her mind.

"Where should I go?" Needleblade asked.

"Return here," she said, giving her location.

She waved the connection closed before he could annoy her more.

. . .

THE VILLAGE DISAPPEARED as they turned the first bend in the road. Willowvine hoped that meant they'd managed to leave without notice.

This road was straighter than the one they traveled yesterday. Not completely straight, but it made a gentle curve that allowed them to see ahead. It was a road they could travel fast. Darkness hid the ground on either side, but Willowvine felt wind on her skin; it was open, at least for now.

"I should check to make sure we aren't being followed," Dawnriver said. "I am not comfortable relying on the hope that Needleblade was busy."

"A good idea," Willowvine said. "I'll go."

"No," Dawnriver said. "I cannot find and return the Stone. You can."

Were they close enough for that to be a concern? "If you find someone following, what will you do?"

"You mean, can I handle myself?" Dawnriver laughed. "Yes. I'm not in your league, but if I think I'm outnumbered, I can ride fast."

Willowvine looked to Springheart and Tom, both riding a little ahead. They'd agreed to walk the horses until there was enough light to see any obstacles. She wanted to get as far away as possible from Needleblade, but there were things Tom couldn't heal and they needed the horses to get to the Library. Too many people had attempted to stop them to let more time pass.

"Don't be long," she said. "We haven't come far, and when dawn makes it safe, we are not waiting for you."

"With luck I will be back before then," he said. "It may take a while to plant some misdirection."

"And if you find we are being pursued?"

"I will do what is necessary."

"Try to avoid killing people," she said. "Too many have died already on this quest and I don't want the Orphan Stone stained with blood when it's placed with the others. Even if they are only bandits."

"I promise," Dawnriver said. He turned his horse and waved as he returned down their path.

Chapter 23

Springheart had half expected Willowvine to order Needleblade's death. It would have changed her, and he was glad she understood the cost of killing. Doing it in a fight was very different from commanding murder.

"How long to the Library?" she asked as she joined them.

"Late tonight if we don't run into problems," Springheart said.

"I should probably learn how to shoot a bow," Tom said. "I don't want to be stuck fighting in so close to an attacker again."

"We can start," Springheart said. "But it's not a skill you can pick up in a few hours. Perhaps when we're done with this quest."

"I'd like that," Tom said. "Do you think we'll adventure again after this?"

"You aren't planning to settle down somewhere safe?" Willowvine asked.

"I like wandering the world. I can do without the plotting and fighting, though," Tom said.

"Me too," Willowvine said. "I haven't given much thought about what comes next."

Springheart had stopped wondering about the future. Too many things could happen to make it dark. He feared a life without Willowvine, knowing she would slip away as she found her place in Elven society.

"Do you think Needleblade gave up?" Tom asked. "He's probably been to the stable already and found that we slipped away."

Springheart shifted his shoulders to release the tension building there.

"We'll know soon enough," Willowvine said. "It won't matter in a little while; we'll have a good enough head start."

"What if he's already coming?" Tom asked. "He has that truth spell. What if he uses it on me?"

"You can't be tricked if you see it coming," Springheart said. "If you see him using herbs, or broken twigs, or seeds, you run."

"Running sounds like the coward's way," Tom said.

"The survivor's way," Willowvine said. "It's foolish to fight every battle you find."

"I'm still going to learn how to fight any battle," Tom said. Then he leaned down to whisper to his horse.

Springheart slowed his own horse a little, wanting some privacy with Willowvine.

"It was a good call to let Dawnriver go," he said. "The man is capable of looking after himself."

"I think he has more skills than we see." She glanced back. "Do you trust him?"

"Do you think they were both trying to stop us?" Springheart had come to trust Dawnriver over the last few days. His actions spoke louder than any suspicion, although the suspicion was still there.

"Just because he's not trying to stop us doesn't mean he is on our side," she said.

"What do you know?" Springheart looked behind them, now more worried.

"Ask him," she said. "I don't want to be the one to tell his story. And I think it's better if Tom didn't hear it from us either."

"When we stop," Springheart said, "I'll make him tell us."

THE SUN WAS BARELY high enough to do more than shed a silver light across the road. It was enough to let the horses move faster than a walk, but Willowvine was holding back. Dawnriver wasn't back yet.

She was still the only person who knew his story. It annoyed her that he hadn't found time to tell Tom and Springheart. The last two days had been hectic, but surely he could have found a few moments to say something.

When he returned, she'd give him a deadline, tell them by the time they reached the Library, or she would. It shouldn't have made a difference, but she was so used to distrust now that his holding back brought up all her early fears.

"He's coming." Tom pointed back down the road.

Willowvine heard the faint beat of hooves. She turned with her hand on her throwing knife. In moments she recognized Dawnriver. He spurred his horse to catch up as he realized they'd seen him. "How did you know?"

Elves had better hearing than humans, and Tom had been the first to identify Dawnriver.

"Lightfoot knew her friend," Tom said, patting the neck of his horse.

"Now you can talk to horses?" Willowvine asked.

"Wouldn't that be great?" he said. "No, I could tell by her reactions."

"Almost as good as speech," Willowvine said. "We'll wait here."

They held the horses waiting the few minutes for Dawn-river to catch up.

"Are we safe?" Willowvine asked.

"Needleblade is still in the village," Dawnriver said. "I laid a few tracks to misdirect him when he decides to look for us. Bloodroot knows what to do to help us."

"Was Needleblade at the stable?" Springheart asked.

"No," Dawnriver said. "He must have gone at midnight and found that we were on the road. So he's plotting something, we can be sure of that."

"We should ride hard," Willowvine said. "The sooner we're off the road the better."

"I can feed the horses energy when we stop," Tom said. "But we need to take short rests to water and feed them, or they won't make the whole journey."

"I can help with that," Dawnriver said. "It will tire us, but we won't slow you down."

"It looks like we have a plan," Willowvine said. "How long can we ride between rests?"

"At full gallop?" Tom asked. "We could stop at every other rest station."

"We'll be at the library before dinner," Dawnriver said. "It will be nice to rest without worrying about being poisoned or attacked."

Willowvine didn't hold out any hope that the attacks would end. The quest wouldn't be over until the Stone was placed in the maze.

"YOU NEED to tell Springheart and Tom who you are," Willowvine said.

They were taking the second rest of the trip and the two healers already looked drawn from keeping the horses fresh.

"It's not a story that can be told in the few minutes we're

standing still." He ran his hand along the pack horse. "These are good steeds."

"Don't change the subject," Willowvine snapped. The stress of the ride was chipping her civilized veneer. "They must trust you."

"When we get to the library," he said. "Or do you think it is more important than getting there?"

"If we are attacked, and they have doubts?"

"That's happened before, and we've survived."

"Why are you so reluctant?"

"Habit. The more people know about our organization, the harder it is to achieve our purposes. We benefit from secrets, so it's important to protect them. It's dangerous for people to know too much."

It must be a very lonely life. "They need to know. If you don't tell them, I'll do it."

"At the next stop, then," he said. "I promise."

Willowvine turned away to get her share of the water and bite of the travel food.

"People?" a woman called out of the trees at the edge of the clearing. "Oh, thank goodness. I've been stranded here since last night."

Willowvine glanced around to make sure everyone was on alert. It didn't sound like Cornflower, but she wasn't going to be fooled again.

An Elven woman stepped from the trees. She looked harmless, but elves were deceptive. That had worked in her favor enough times when people dismissed her as being too young, or too slight, to be a threat. When the woman joined them, Willowvine could see more details. Her clothes were rumpled, but not torn. Her hair was escaping an intricate braid. She limped slightly as she approached.

"What happened?" Willowvine asked. She held up her hand to stop Tom running over to heal the woman.

"Bandits. They stole the horses and took my companions. I was walking among the trees and managed to hide until they rode off."

"Where were you going?" Willowvine asked.

"The university," she said, then wiped her hand on her dress. "Where are my manners, my name is Lilyflame."

Willowvine introduced her party and offered food. "Will someone realize you are missing? A place you were expected?" It was not where they headed, but there were a few settlements before it would be obvious that their destination was the Library.

"It will take them days to find her," Springheart said. "We can take you to the next village. You can send a bird from there."

"Are you hurt?" Tom asked stepping forward. "I'm a healer."

"That is so kind of you," Lilyflame said. "I am just tired. I think you need to save your strength in case there's a real injury."

Willowvine moved away from the group. Dawnriver stood by the horses, watching the action. Knowing she'd lost the chance to leave the woman behind, she settled on getting them on the road as quickly as possible.

"We won't be able to move as fast," Dawnriver said.

"It's only until we can drop her off," Willowvine said. "The village is only a few minutes off the main road." She remembered the journey away from the Library when they'd sealed the Well.

"That just seems a little convenient," he said. "Just as we are making progress, something happens to slow us down."

"She's just a stranded elf," Willowvine said. "We've had problems with bandits too. Perhaps the same ones who took and slaughtered our horses attacked here. Your work has made you suspect everyone."

"And I'm still alive," he said. "Her presence also makes it difficult for me to tell Springheart and Tom who I am."

"Almost like you arranged it that way," Willowvine said. She laughed at his expression and nudged him. "See, you aren't the only one who can make a conspiracy out of whole cloth."

Chapter 24

Willowvine asked Lilyflame to loosen her grip around her waist. When they'd started out, she'd been calm, but when the horses sped up, Lilyflame had leaned in and tightened her hold.

"Can we slow down a little?" Lilyflame asked, releasing from a death grip to a tight hold.

"If the bandits are still in the area, we should not linger. If you squeeze the breath out of me, we'll both fall." Reminding her of the bandits who'd attacked her was enough to overcome Lilyflame's fear of falling off the horse.

"Will you ride the whole way like this?" she asked.

"As much as we can," Willowvine said. "We are in a hurry."

"When you leave me, where will you go?"

"Our destination is past the village, don't worry. Dropping you off is only a small delay."

Lilyflame clutched Willowvine tighter as the horse found more energy at the sight of a long straight stretch. Willowvine felt its excitement hum through her body; perhaps she was riding a retired racer. Even knowing he'd need rest sooner didn't make Willowvine rein him in. The rush of speed was exhilarating. And it stopped the woman behind her talking.

Tom, Dawnriver, and Springheart whooped and urged their horses into a race. For the first time in many days, Willowvine felt joy rushing through her with no shadow of fear or suspicion.

The road ahead turned all too soon. The horses slowed on their own, or perhaps Tom had given some silent command. Willowvine was not entirely convinced that Tom couldn't speak to them.

"I hope that didn't cause injuries," Lilyflame said when they slowed to a canter.

"They are built to run like that," Willowvine said. "A smooth road is perfect. Horses get injured on uneven ground."

"Of course, you would know more than I," Lilyflame said. "My usual travel is by carriage. When I say usual, I mean the few times I have journeyed anywhere. I shall probably stay home after this adventure."

"A pity," Willowvine said. "Travel brings excitement. What stories will you have to tell your grandchildren if you stay at home?"

Lilyflame loosened her hold on Willowvine's waist. Something crackled and Willowvine caught the scent of roses and pine.

"Your destination must be important for you to push your animals this way," Lilyflame said.

"Where we go today may not be the last stop on our mission."

"Oh, not merely an adventure?"

Willowvine wanted the conversation over, but something drew words from her. Perhaps it was weariness at lying and avoiding conversations to keep secrets. "Yes," she said. "That's why we can only leave you at the next village."

"There are many places on this road you could go to,"

Lilyflame said. "If you are willing to cross mountains and deserts, the entire world is ahead of you."

"We may have to do those very things," Willowvine said. It couldn't hurt to tell Lilyflame where they were headed. The world might be ahead of them, but she wouldn't need much effort to deduce the Library as their stop. And if knowing that shut Lilyflame up, it would be worth the risk.

"I hope you will rest before taking such a terrifying step into the unknown," Lilyflame said.

"We will be stopping at the Library," Willowvine said. "Who knows where we will go from there." She nudged the horse to go faster.

Lilyflame hugged her closer and didn't speak.

The ride had been silent for as long as it took to find a resting place. The full out gallop meant they were between the official areas when Tom called a halt.

Willowvine waited until Lilyflame dismounted and rode her horse to the stream where Tom and Dawnriver were attending the animals.

"Damage?" she asked.

"They are tired," Tom said. "No injuries, so we will be fine when they've been watered and fed."

"Have extra food yourself," she said. "We don't need to ration, as we'll be at the Library soon enough."

"How is our passenger?" Dawnriver asked. "Do you know anything more about her?"

"Not yet," she said. "Join us when you're done. I plan to ask her more questions now that we are away from where she was attacked."

Willowvine no longer felt a need to feed Lilyflame's curiosity. She wondered if the lack of caution earlier was due to being so close to the woman. She was guileless, or seemed to be, and her innocence was out of place with her age. It was possible she was simply the sheltered daughter of an important elf. But with distance, Willowvine's suspicious nature resurfaced.

Springheart was standing near Lilyflame, handing her the spare water skins.

"Could you fill them?" he asked.

"Yes, of course I'll help," Lilyflame said. She looked at the seals and then back at him.

He twisted the corks out. "Just about three quarters full," he said.

Willowvine watched as she walked toward the stream. "How does someone that age not know how to open a water bottle?"

"There are some very spoiled elves," he said. "She probably has servants to do everything for her."

"You trust her with our water?"

He grinned. "Not for a minute. I'll test the contents when she comes back. If she's done anything to the water, we'll know there's something wrong with her."

"And if she hasn't?"

"Then we'll still only suspect there's something wrong." He dug out the sack of travel bread. "We're going to arrive at the Library hungry."

"We've been hungry before," she said. "Tom and Dawnriver need more of this than we do. Something has to replenish them after they give the horses power."

Lilyflame returned, the water skins bulging with the corks only half inserted.

Springheart took them and thanked her. He walked toward Tom and Dawnriver the sack of travel bread in his hands.

"Are you hungry?" Willowvine asked Lilyflame.

"A little, but we'll be at the village soon. I don't want to take your food. You'll need it on your journey."

Willowvine broke her serving in half. "We will be able to

buy more." She hoped it was true, but they had little they could afford to sell.

Lilyflame took the bread and nibbled.

"It must have been frightening for you," Willowvine said.

Lilyflame swallowed the morsel of bread. "The attack? Yes. It was. The roads are not safe any longer. The world is changing. I don't think it's getting better, do you?"

"I've found the world to be as it is, better or worse is in how you react to it."

"That's so brave of you." She leaned in as though to share a secret. "I know the men are happy to take risks, but you should be careful. You should insist on traveling only during daylight. The thought that you might be on the road at night, with bandits on the prowl, frightens me."

"Thank you for your concern," Willowvine said. "We spend little time traveling at night. I assure you, any bandits we encounter will regret it."

Chapter 25

It had been difficult to convince them to rest again. Rainblossom was running out of time. She felt a kernel of sympathy with her agent. These people fought any attempt to move them off course.

Now they were checking all the horses after she'd sworn that she saw signs of damage to the pack animal. One that no one rode and no one watched.

"I need to stretch my legs," she said. "I won't be long."

She slipped away before anyone could stop her.

A little way into the woods, she came on a clearing next to a lake so deep its waters were almost black.

"Needleblade?" she called quietly. There was no answer. It didn't surprise her. Following them while staying off the road was no easy feat.

She held the crystal in her ring at eye level and called his name again.

"I am almost there," he said. "It will be faster if I don't have to speak."

Insolence. It was better than incompetence. She described the clearing and told him to hurry.

While she waited, Rainblossom paced. She needed a plan. One that would help her defeat Springheart and Willowvine. And one that could go into effect now.

She couldn't kill them; they were too skilled with weapons. And she couldn't persuade them to join her for the night, but she needed to delay them somehow.

A rustle in the undergrowth broke her concentration. She reached for her knife, before remembering she'd left it behind in support of her alias. Lilyflame was not the kind of elf who went armed.

Needleblade stepped into the clearing, leading his horse. Both elf and animal were exhausted. The horse might not make it much farther, but she would ride it to death if that's what it took to beat Willowvine.

"Were you able to find out where they are going?" he asked, letting the animal's reins drop so it could drink from the edge of the lake.

"Yes, but it was not a surprise. The Library," she said. "They are still looking for clues. We need to misdirect them and find the Stone ourselves."

"How will we do that? Are they taking you there?"

This moment was why she agreed to let him follow them after he fought her orders to leave the mission to her. He would be of use to the plan in a way other than spy.

"No, but one of us must hurry ahead."

"Me? I can do the research," he said. Looking over at his horse, he added, "You will need to slow them a little to give me time."

"Tom seems to be the weakest," she said. "He is using what little energy he has for the horses."

"He's just a human boy," Needleblade said. "Perhaps you can use something to drain him faster. They will stop for his sake."

"Perhaps something like that would work," she said. "They

will not be persuaded. Willowvine is able to block the effect of my spells. I should have been able to pull the whole truth from her, but only got the destination, and that cloaked in a lie. I fail to understand their secrecy when it would be obvious even to a blind man."

"How will you do it?"

She glanced around, a plan forming in her mind. "Do you have a weapon I can conceal?"

"You plan to kill one of them?" He undid the belt holding his short sword in its ornate sheath. "The two healers are strong. Injuring one will not stop them. Cornflower's attack should have sent Willowvine to the next life, but she yet fights on."

Rainblossom took the belt and drew the short sword. Most elves carried them. Hers was left behind in her rooms. The shine on the edge of the blade showed that Needleblade kept his weapon sharp and clean.

She looked at Needleblade. He was tired enough that he wasn't thinking. She let the sheath and belt fall to the ground and thrust the sword into his belly.

He looked down at the wound, surprised.

She pulled the sword loose and thrust again, this time into his heart.

Needleblade crumpled at her feet.

"Healers have not yet found a way to reverse that," she said.

She dropped her scarf into the pool of blood, then dragged Needleblade's body toward the lake, dropping him when the horse whinnied and sidestepped, nervous at the scent of death.

She coaxed the animal aside and tossed the reins over a low branch. She had no time for finesse; the others would come searching soon.

Needleblade's body was heavy, but she managed to haul it into the water. She smiled as she watched him sink below the surface. The body would float soon, but perhaps not soon enough for Willowvine to see him.

She pulled the blanket from its place behind the horse's saddle and wiped her arms clean. Then she scrubbed at the blood on the rocks at the edge of the lake.

No time to do a proper job, she thought. Dipping the blanket in the water, she wrung it out to sluice away the last red stains. Then the blanket joined Needleblade.

Rainblossom sheathed the sword and wrapped the belt around her waist. The horse was still nervous, but she managed to mount him. She kicked him into a gallop. A sharp angle would take her past the rest area behind the trees and onto the road.

The horse might not make it to the Library, but close was better than nothing, perhaps all she needed was a head start.

"WE CAN'T WAIT ANY LONGER," Willowvine said. She glared at the trees where Lilyflame had disappeared as if her will would bring her back. "I don't care how much she wants to stretch her legs, we must find her and get going."

"Tom and Dawnriver can stay with the horses," Springheart said. "We'll look together."

"Good. Too many bandits around for us to split up too much." She handed her pouch to Dawnriver, wanting to move as swiftly as possible. "Do you have weapons?"

"I did stop to acquire a few knives when we were in town," Dawnriver said. He picked up a leather bag and reached into a pocket on the side. "It doesn't take a lot of skill to throw one. Tom and I will be fine."

She considered leaving Springheart to protect Tom and taking Dawnriver with her. But she knew it would slow the search if she did. Springheart knew her well enough that they didn't always need to speak to get the job done. If they found

Lilyflame in need of a healer, they would carry her back to the clearing.

"We won't be long," she said. "I don't think she would have gone too far. She's afraid of her shadow."

Willowvine followed Springheart at a run. Lilyflame's tracks were easy to find, at least that was a benefit of her inexperience with travel. Any elf used to the road would have been hard, if not impossible, to track.

"Do you hear that?" Springheart said, coming to a stop.

Willowvine shifted her concentration from the ground ahead. A faint bird call; someone was hurt and attracting carrion birds. "We have a few minutes by the sound."

The tracks were still clear.

They raced toward the call of the carrion bird. Willowvine regretted her assumption that Lilyflame was dawdling. Of course, she would want to leave as quickly as possible. Her annoyance turned to fear that the woman's injuries were going to slow them down.

They burst into a clearing. Across the way, a mountain lake lay dark and silent. Edged by rocky shelves, it was the kind that didn't taper off into deeps but simply dropped away.

"Willowvine," Springheart called.

He was bending over a flutter of blue in the middle of the clearing. Willowvine joined him and saw it was one of Lilyflame's scarves. A silky blue scrap of fabric soaked with blood.

"It's too much," she said. "No one could survive this."

"She didn't." Springheart pointed.

Drag marks led to the edge of the lake. They would not find Lilyflame's body.

"This wasn't bandits," she said. "They wouldn't bother hiding their actions."

"We need to go," Springheart said. "We'll stop at the village and report this."

"I should ride ahead to the Library. We can't let anything delay us now. Whoever is trying to stop us...it's getting worse."

"We stay together," Springheart said. "It's safer with more of us. If you go, who would watch your back?"

His plan was the right one, Willowvine knew in her rational mind. Her instinct said they were too late. But if she was killed on the way, there would be no catching up. The Stone would be lost forever. No one else would care enough.

Leafcreek would die disappointed.

SPRINGHEART RODE BEHIND, he'd said, to watch for anyone approaching that way, but it was to keep his eye on Willowvine. He'd seen the conflict in her when she'd agreed to stay with them. He was afraid she'd leave them behind if anything else happened. He couldn't lose her now. The Stone was too important and there were too many people trying to stop them.

Tom had agreed that if they didn't gallop the whole way, they could bypass the rest areas — at least the next few. Springheart could feel his own horse tire beneath him, but the animal kept up the canter as if he also knew the urgency of their mission.

When they'd come to the turnoff for the village, Dawnriver had volunteered to report and then catch up. He'd travel faster and if they slowed a little, he would not have to ruin his horse to rejoin them.

Springheart heard a single horse approach from the side. He reached for his bow, nocking an arrow and aiming toward the sound.

Dawnriver broke through the trees lining the road. "They showed me a short cut," he shouted.

Willowvine turned in her saddle. "What will they do?"

"There is no official there. A few humans agreed to look at the clearing and try to fish up any evidence. They say the lake doesn't give back what goes in, that there's a deep current that flows through the mountain, but they will try. They sent a rider to another village where there's a constable to take the information."

"We've done what we can," Springheart said.

Tom's horse reared.

"Arrow!" Dawnriver shouted.

Another landed on the road between Springheart and Dawnriver. The horses sidestepped in an effort to get away.

"To the trees," Springheart said.

Before anyone could move, another arrow flew. This time it didn't land harmlessly. It struck Dawnriver in the throat.

Tom leapt from his horse and ran to Dawnriver's side as the elf slid from the saddle. He laid a hand on the horse and it calmed and stood as shelter from the attack.

He reached for Dawnriver's throat. "It's not fatal," he said.

He pulled out a knife and sawed the arrow in half while Dawnriver held the shaft still at the wound. Then he whispered something to Dawnriver, reached around the back of his neck and yanked the arrow through.

Springheart turned his attention to the road. Willowvine was walking back to them. No more arrows flew.

"They're gone," she said.

Chapter 26

Willowvine helped pull Dawnriver into the shade of the trees lining the road. It didn't feel safe, but they had to deal with his wound, and the middle of the road was too exposed.

"Can you heal him?" she asked Tom.

"Yes," he said. "It's a complicated healing. I won't have anything left to keep the horses going."

"He's more important right now," she said. "We'll find another way when you're done."

She watched as Tom knelt beside Dawnriver. The wound was bleeding and she didn't see how it could be so easily healed. If the attackers wanted to delay them, they'd succeeded. Now they wouldn't limp through the Library gates until long into the night. Another day would pass before any clues revealed themselves.

Springheart was pacing, his bow ready with an arrow. She closed her eyes and sent her senses into the area. "There's no one here," she called to him.

He joined them, looking down as Tom finished his work.

"That's the best I can do now," Tom said. "Can you travel, Dawnriver?"

Dawnriver opened his mouth but only a wheeze came through. Tom bent to touch him but was waved away.

Willowvine reached to hold Dawnriver's hands so Tom could do his work, but he batted her away, too. He looked down at the soft earth and pulled out his own knife. Then, using the blade he scratched a message in the dirt. Time. Later.

Tom sat back on his heels. "Will you be okay on a horse?" Dawnriver nodded.

"Do you mean it will heal with time?" Willowvine asked.

Dawnriver nodded again.

"I think we should be on our way," Willowvine said. "It's going to take hours." She wished she'd gone ahead earlier. Maybe they wouldn't be in this position if she wasn't with them.

"You should go now," Springheart said. "Is there a way to refresh her horse without killing ours?"

Willowvine thought for a moment she'd imagined the words. Springheart was sending her alone? "Isn't it more dangerous?"

"Be careful. Move fast. We'll be along later." He started unloading her horse. "Less weight will help."

Willowvine turned to Tom and Dawnriver. They were pointing and having some silent argument. "What's wrong?"

"I can take a little energy from each of us and transfer it to your horse. We'll go slowly but you can ride hard without killing him," Tom said.

"Why are you arguing?" She knew Tom was keeping something from her. If only Dawnriver could speak, maybe she could get the whole story.

"Dawnriver is worried that we won't have enough energy to heal if something else happens."

"Is he right?"

"Yes, but someone is trying to stop us getting to the

Library," Tom said. "One of us needs to go. You are the lightest and you know more about what we are looking for."

"And if someone gets hurt..." she couldn't bring herself to say any more.

"Traveling fast makes it hard to be on the defensive," Springheart said. He handed her a chunk of travel bread and a water skin. "We'll be in a better position to stay safe."

She looked from one to the other of her companions. This was what she wanted, but they hadn't thought it through. If one of them died because of her, how would she survive the guilt?

Tom beckoned her over. "Link hands." He took her left hand in his and used his other to touch the flank of her horse.

Willowvine felt warmth flow through her. Some drained through Tom to the horse, but some stayed. When he released her, Tom sagged.

"Willowvine, go." Springheart gave her a shove toward the horse.

She sprang into the saddle and urged it to a gallop.

IT WAS dark as she rode through the gates of the Library. A figure slipped from the shadows, bringing a lantern. Her horse staggered but took a final few steps forward.

"I've been expecting you," the figure said. The shape resolved into an elf who was probably as old as Leafcreek. "Stonerose sent a bird to tell us you were on your way."

She slid to the ground, knees bending in an effort to remain standing. "There was trouble on the road."

"You are safe here," he said. "I'm Cloudseed."

"If you were my worst enemy, I couldn't fight you off," she said. "The horse?"

"He'll be tended to," Cloudseed said. "Where are the others?"

"Coming. I need to start searching the records."

Cloudseed supported her and started walking to the gate as a boy ran across to take the reins.

"You need food and rest," Cloudseed said. "I started the search, but you are too worn to hear my findings."

It's bad news, she thought. No matter how tired she was, he would have given her good news. "I can't waste time."

"I assure you this will not be wasted time," Cloudseed said. "An hour. Our healer will attend you, but some things need time."

"No more than an hour," she mumbled. "We are being pursued."

"We will talk when you are not asleep on your feet."

WILLOWVINE BLINKED HER EYES OPEN. When had she fallen asleep? No light shone through the small window, so it hadn't been long. She sat and heard someone slip from the room, footsteps rapidly fading.

The Library healers had done their job. She stretched and stood. The weariness was gone, along with all the chafing and bruises a hard ride delivered.

Someone approached her small chamber. She sought a weapon from instinct, then stopped. This was a safe place. She had to believe that.

Her visitor coaxed a glow from an ettran stone. Cloudseed smiled at her. "You look much better."

"Thank you for this," she said. "I can't linger. Our quest is under attack."

He sat on a wooden chair covered in intricate carvings of animals and plants. All the furnishings were decorated with embroidered scenes, or carvings of old legends.

"I know," he said, looking down at the floor. "An Elven woman came only a few hours before you. She seemed refined and civilized. A fellow scholar. Then I refused to allow her to see the research I set aside for you."

Yet another rival for the Stone? "Who was she?"

"Her name is Rainblossom," Cloudseed said. "She became angry at first and then agreed to do her own research. I left her in a section of the library that held some of our oldest books. I should have stayed and watched her."

Willowvine felt her muscles tense. This Rainblossom had done something awful if Cloudseed had trouble speaking of it. "And?"

"She broke into the room I'd set aside for you. She threw most of the documents on the floor and drowned them in water — a spell, I think. A book survived, one that I hadn't thought so important. She'd torn out pages and left the rest on the table."

No wonder he wanted her refreshed when she heard. Willowvine knew she wouldn't have had the strength to bear the news. "Does that mean we are lost?"

"It will take time," Cloudseed said. "Time you don't have. We can restore the knowledge in the sodden pages. But the ones she took? That is gone unless you can find them, and they are not destroyed."

"How long have I been here?" She glanced at the window again. Still no sign of dawn.

"A little over an hour."

The others would not get to her in time. Willowvine knew she had to make the choices now. There must be hope. "Can I see the remaining pages?"

Chapter 27

The room had been cleared of all the destroyed documents. Willowvine assumed someone, or perhaps a team of people, worked in a private room inside the Library to undo the damage. She wished them success; lost information was damage to the past and the future.

The room contained a fireplace, unlit, a small stone table, two stools, and five ettran lanterns. Studying here would not be dependent on the sun.

Willowvine joined Cloudseed at the table, ignoring the stool. She took the cotton gloves he passed her but let him handle the book.

"It's small. I wonder why she didn't take it with her," she said.

"I think we are to read a message in the destruction. Taking the book alone would put your quest in danger. Destroying what she did was a message to us, the librarians."

"Why? Elves revere knowledge."

"Perhaps a time is coming when that will change." Cloudseed lay the book open at the torn pages. "See, here, she did not make a clean cut. There are still words left near the spine."

Willowvine leaned in close. "Evil. And this looks like part of a word," she said her finger hovering over the letters.

"Beast? Feast? Least?" Cloudseed fluttered his fingers above the torn edges.

Willowvine saw the glow of a spell, but nothing came clearer. "What about the other pages?" Rainblossom had taken five sheets from the book.

Cloudseed gently moved the fragments of paper. "Just single letters." He turned to the last one. "Stone?" he asked.

The diagonal tear left the last three letters entire, but she saw there was at least one, perhaps two more in the word. "It could be, but what use is it to find words? We need meanings."

"Yes," Cloudseed said. "I don't think we can be sure about the meaning without much more of the book."

Willowvine reached for the book and closed it before looking along the page edges, trying to see if the tearing was hiding cleaner cuts. Were other pages missing? She couldn't find evidence of secret damage. "What is this book?"

Cloudseed took it back and turned it to look at the front cover. "A diary," he said. "Centuries old."

"Why did you add it to the collection for me to review?"

"It comes from the time when the Stone of Orphan disappeared. I thought we might find a mention."

"If there are passages about the Orphan Stone, would it just be on those pages?"

"Perhaps there are hints in the sheets left." Cloudseed opened the book again. This time, starting a few pages before the damage. "Yes, here. 'The army is preparing for the invasion,'" he read. "'Once again the passage between worlds opens. Will we be overrun this time? Will it be a peaceful people, or a warrior horde?'"

"The Well at the Center of the World." The memory of the voice coming out of the darkness tightened her muscles as though making ready to flee. Fear swept over her as though she was still in the battle. "I think that first word must be beast."

"It says that the sun is almost touching the stones." Cloudseed pointed. "Look at how he writes the word."

She saw how the s and t were formed. Turning the page back, they found a mark next to the rip. The other word fragment must be stone. "Does it say anything about the Stones of Power?"

Cloudseed read in silence, his lips moving as though he was arguing the meaning with a colleague.

Willowvine paced the room. Waiting was doing nothing to help her, but everything to help Rainblossom. "Did anyone see the woman ride out?" If she could follow a trail, perhaps it wasn't too late.

"No," Cloudseed said, still reading. "Of course!"

Willowvine spun to face him. "What? Is there something I can use?"

His face split into a grin. "Oh, yes. The woman should have taken the entire book."

"Well?" Patience was not something she could afford.

"It is scattered over several pages, but I know how to link passages, and the vandal did not. After the invasion, when the Scree arrived, the council thought the approach to the Well should be fortified. There was much debate as usual, but eventually, they moved the Orphan Stone to replace one of the originals. It seemed to calm the beast for longer."

"So, instead of being bad luck, orphans have brought peace," she said. A wave of disgust and frustration choked any further words for a moment. "Why was it kept secret?"

"Perhaps they feared someone would move the other Stones of Power. If they did, no one could predict the result," Cloudseed said.

"And if we take it back to the Guardian?"

"The beast is dead," Cloudseed said. "I see no reason to fear removing it."

It wasn't far to the Well. The road wandered a little as though the builder didn't really want to reach the destination. But Willowvine knew the shortcuts, and that would be an advantage. The darkness wasn't much of a problem for her, but a horse might stumble.

"I'm leaving," she said. "When the others arrive, tell them where I've gone. Springheart will know how to find me."

"To the Well? You can't go alone," Cloudseed said. "Whoever this Rainblossom is, if she's willing to destroy knowledge, she won't hesitate to kill you."

Willowvine checked her belt for her knives. They were missing. "I can defend myself. I only need my weapons."

"They are in the room where you rested."

"I must go immediately," she said, running to the door.

"How long before your companions arrive?" Cloudseed followed her as she rushed to find her belongings.

"Possibly a few hours. And your healers will need to work on one of them. Springheart can leave Tom and Dawnriver here."

"Will he be in any condition to ride?"

"By the time he comes, I'll be waiting for help with the Stone, or I'll be dead." She strapped on the belt, slung her bow across her shoulders, and added a quiver of arrows.

"When did Rainblossom leave?" Willowvine asked as she pulled on her boots.

"Only a short while before you arrived."

"Did she take a horse?"

"No. They were all in the stable. If she'd tried to take one, we could have stopped her here."

"Do you think she knows how to find the Well?"

"I would say not easily," Cloudseed said. "It is supposition, but few people bypass us and go directly there. She was a stranger. No one would have told her the way."

"Then she probably took the road," Willowvine said. "That is in our favor."

"If I can't convince you to stay, I wish you safe journey. Perhaps it is time for us to entertain soldiers at the Library. We are defenseless, as you see."

"Perhaps," Willowvine said. "But the beast is dead. I'll rescue the Orphan Stone, so unless there are other treasures hidden at the Well, you should be safe."

"I would have said there were none yesterday." Cloudseed hurried beside her to the door. "But perhaps we should commence a new field of study."

Willowvine laughed and waved goodbye as she slipped through the gate and into the night.

Chapter 28

Rainblossom stood at the first stone in the spiral path leading to the Well. She knew the beast was dead and the Well no longer lay open to other worlds, but she could feel the power of the place. The maze lay in a shallow depression, ringed by mounds that couldn't be natural, and even if they were, it was like a bowl slowly filling with power. What would happen when it filled?

She'd hoped that the Orphan Stone would look different from the others, but the entire path seemed to be made of identical pavers. She should have taken the book. The joy she'd felt in destroying any clue about the Stones had burned bright and fast. Now she was here with nothing but a few torn pages to help her with the last act.

As the sun rose above the hills in the distance, she saw more detail. At least she had time. Willowvine and her friends must still be trying to get to the Library.

A breeze freshened the air, waking her senses and highlighting her fatigue. Rainblossom faced the sun and closed her eyes. She was tired, but it was almost over. She could rest soon and then start rebuilding the world. The Stone of Orphan would be at the bottom of the sea, safe from any rescue.

An owl cried. She opened her eyes to see the bird swoop across from one mound to another. These moments of change, when the dark gave way to the light, and night creatures hurried home to hide from the day creatures, gave her a sense of peace. She could draw some energy into her body, enough to get her through the next steps.

An arrow clipped her sleeve.

She turned slowly, unwilling to show fear. The girl stood at the edge of the trees. "Why don't you die? I sent my best archers after you. I see I should have just killed you myself."

"Lilyflame?" Willowvine said. "Who did you kill at the lake?"

Did she truly think she was facing that vapid elf? "Needle-blade had served his purpose. Well, he'd failed, but as a diversion when I needed to get away, he was useful."

"And which is your real name? Rainblossom? Lilyflame? Or are they both a lie?"

"Rainblossom is my true name; you will never be able to use it again," she said. "How did you know to come here?"

"You thought you destroyed all clues? No."

The girl inched closer, bow raised, an arrow ready to fly.

"Unfortunate. Perhaps I will go back and take out my anger on the rest of the Library."

"You won't get the chance," Willowvine said.

"Why did you miss? You could have sent that arrow into my heart."

"I wanted you to face me," Willowvine said. "I would rather not kill you."

Rainblossom laughed. "You think you can capture me?"

"Why are you doing this?"

"Because the world needs to change, and I want it to

change in my favor." Rainblossom looked to the trees behind Willowvine. "Your companions can come out."

"They aren't there," Willowvine said. "Why don't you give me the pages you stole?"

"You're alone?" She laughed; this girl was arrogant. "Do you think you can make me give you the clues to the Stone?"

WILLOWVINE DROPPED HER BOW. It was a distance weapon, and she needed to get in close.

Rainblossom held out the papers torn from the book. "I'll burn these," she said. "Step back. Leave here and you'll live."

If the pages contained the location of the Stone, she couldn't let them burn. There were too many here to test them all. "Does it matter?" Willowvine asked, stalling for time. "If you die, we have all the time in the world to find the Orphan Stone. If you win, I'm not sure how long you will let me live."

She took a step forward. Could she snatch the pages before Rainblossom reacted?

"I don't want to kill you," Rainblossom said, her emotions gone. "Not now that I will possess the Stone. Before, yes. I charged Cornflower with the task. Needleblade was too weak. It surprised me that she was the same. I thought she would value the money we promised. Perhaps she knew it was a lie. She did not survive to find out. It seems bandits don't take kindly to betrayal."

"Or the money wasn't enough," Willowvine said. "What will you do with the Orphan Stone?"

"The Stones must not be disturbed. It was belief before, but belief can change. I was going to drop it into the sea, but now that I am certain the Orphan Stone is here, I understand more. The Stone is keeping this world safe."

Willowvine realized Rainblossom was caught in her own

revelation. She darted forward, knife ready. At the last second, Rainblossom stepped aside and tripped Willowvine.

"You are so easy to fool," Rainblossom said, laughing.

Willowvine rolled onto her back, blade extended to defend against attack. "Only one time," she said.

Rainblossom stood closer to the Well, her back to Willowvine, no weapon in sight.

Gaining her feet, Willowvine stepped forward, closing the distance, but staying just out of reach. She wouldn't fall for any trick again. She still had a chance to capture Rainblossom. Killing in this place might trigger catastrophe.

"If you don't want to kill people, who sent the attacks?" she asked.

Keeping her eyes on Rainblossom, Willowvine inched closer.

"Oh, that. I ordered them to miss," Rainblossom said. "Until the last. It was just to slow you."

Willowvine watched as Rainblossom took a step. She was walking the path of the stones. It was clear that she knew nothing about this place. That might be useful in stopping her. Rainblossom either had reinforcements on the way or didn't see Willowvine as a threat. It was a weakness that Willowvine would exploit.

"Where do you think the Stone is?" Willowvine asked. They were halfway through the path now.

"I'll know when I step on it," Rainblossom said.

That hadn't helped the last time Willowvine fought here. This time, every step she took toward the center brought vivid memories of the beast and the torment.

"It's not the only stone of power here," she said. "We used another to defeat the beast."

"Then this will be dismantled when I win. So much power should not be concentrated in one place."

"It kept the beast quiet for long periods," Willowvine said. "Would you have us invaded more often?"

Rainblossom spun and flung a handful of herbs her way.

Willowvine twisted to dodge them, but they followed. She felt her body grow numb and then her legs collapsed under her.

Rainblossom stood over her, hands full of spell ingredients. "Stay there," she said. "I may have need of you when I find the Stone."

Willowvine could barely force her lungs to pull in air. She couldn't argue, or agree, or warn the woman.

Chapter 29

Rainblossom bent to stare into Willowvine's eyes. "Perhaps it was too much. I will need you alive." She crushed a leaf with her left ring finger and thumb. A clean scent filled the air and then the stench of decayed flesh defiled it.

She reached forward and painted Willowvine's lips with the juice. The girl drew in a deep breath and color returned to her face.

"Why do you want to destroy the Stone?" Willowvine asked her.

"If you are trying to delay until help arrives, it won't work," Rainblossom said. It was clear to the people in her faction, why couldn't everyone see the signs? "I told you I don't want to destroy it any longer."

"I thought that was a lie." She took a breath. "My friends are too far behind. I'm not delaying. I really want to know."

If she could convince Willowvine of the truth, she would be a valuable ally. The orphan had survived more than most elves. Her skills would be valuable if directed to the right actions.

"Our world is in danger," Rainblossom said. "The invasions, as you call them, were a way of clearing out the weaknesses in our society. We could not stop them building this." She waved her arm to encompass the path and the Well. "Once complete, it was too powerful to destroy."

"How do you know this?" Willowvine asked.

Rainblossom lowered herself to sit beside the girl. "I studied histories and I possess the clarity of mind needed to finish this. I can make, and act on, decisions that no one else will. I'm...accomplished and far more intelligent than people who disagree with me. We have many books that tell of the time they built this, but they ostracized the dissenters. We had no knowledge of how it was created. The builders only worked on parts, only a few had the whole plan. They destroyed the documentation. And the few...they died quickly over the following years."

"Do you know how we defeated the beast?" Willowvine asked.

"You were lucky," Rainblossom said. "We can lure another when it is time."

WILLOWVINE CONCENTRATED ON moving her fingers. They were underneath her, and Rainblossom wouldn't see her efforts. At first, the spell took all sensation away, but the antidote that let her breathe and speak had given her enough feeling back she could sense her body, just not move it. Starting with her fingers seemed the best option. If she managed to free them, she would work on the other muscles.

"It wasn't luck," Willowvine said. But had it been? Was it luck that the prophecy brought Madeline to this world in time to kill the beast? Was it luck that they found all the clues at just the right moment?

"Luck comes in many forms," Rainblossom said. She rose to her feet.

Willowvine couldn't let her walk away. If Rainblossom found the Orphan Stone, there would be no way to stop her. Her plans seemed to change each time she answered a question. Whatever the real plot, the elves were in danger. "Did you know that the other Stones are drifting?" The secret would be out if Willowvine failed.

Rainblossom smiled at the news. "You see? Cartref agrees. Our world is telling us the Stones are no longer important."

That wasn't what Leafcreek thought, and as the Guardian, his interpretation was more likely true. But when you dealt with a world, you didn't exactly get a clear answer.

"Or hope is lost," Willowvine said. Her little finger rubbed against the ground. She'd never been grateful for a scrape in her life. Once the finger moved, she felt her body responding. She had to delay Rainblossom. "But you may be right."

"WE WILL ONLY KNOW when it is over," Rainblossom said. She looked through the pages again. There was no more on them than before. Why would the author bother to write all of this, and not the exact location?

"Did your people move the Stone of Abundance?"

Willowvine was standing, but she didn't hold the knife. Rainblossom could tell the girl wasn't fully recovered. She swayed lightly as though pushed by the breeze. That spell should have held her for hours. What kind of magic did she wield?

"To the quarry?" Rainblossom asked. She thought through the ingredients she had for another spell, but without a guarantee it would be effective, she decided to save her effort. "We did," she said. "Although we didn't record the location. We made an attempt to slow the spread of elves. A small population is more united. Now, elves care about humans and fay, and goblins. Even Scree are invited to research along with us now that they say they've forsaken violence."

"Hard to believe they can keep that promise," Willowvine said.

She no longer swayed, but still made no move forward.

"Another thing we must leave to time. But if we are right, my faction, then scattering the Stones is right. This one we can send to the bottom of the ocean. The other two can sink into the ground if that is what Cartref wants." The belief that their world was sentient seemed undeniable to most, but the world never spoke to her, so Rainblossom doubted it.

"What about me?" Willowvine said. "Will orphans still be exiled? It is more unfair now that we know the truth."

"No elf will be cast out," Rainblossom said. "Why would I do that? If the elves are to regain their prominence, then all of us must be together." The stupid girl sold her loyalty for such a low price. It was all about acceptance for her, not about the future of her people.

"Then let me help you," Willowvine said, taking a step toward her. "I've fought and won here before."

WILLOWVINE WALKED SLOWLY TOWARD RAINBLOSSOM. Her plan was working. The woman looked at her differently, more like an opportunity than an inconvenience. All without lying. Perhaps she was learning to be more like an elf; all Rainblossom's assumptions came from thin air.

She slid her hand into the pocket that held her throwing knife, pretending her hip hurt from the fall.

Rainblossom continued to pace the stones to the center. Waiting for a moment on each to see if it announced itself as the Orphan Stone.

"If I don't reveal the Stone before we reach the center, we

must think of something else. It's good that we have time," Rainblossom said.

They stood only a few circles out from the well. Willowvine could feel the evil from the last time she stood here. The beast may be dead, but what happened here left its mark.

"I can try something," she said. "I just thought of it."

Rainblossom paid no attention to her bluff.

Willowvine ran, passing Rainblossom and turning to confront her. She raised her knife. "I can't let you win."

Rainblossom tossed the pages away. "No one will win if I lose." She darted toward Willowvine, fists already swinging.

Willowvine ducked under her arms, slicing deeply at the woman's side.

"How could you betray me like this?" Rainblossom held her arm to the wound, blood oozing down her clothes. "You said you would help." With one sweep of her free arm, Rainblossom tossed seeds and twigs into the air.

Willowvine was already moving before she released the spell. She held her breath and avoided the wounded woman until the air cleared.

"You said you didn't want to kill to get the Stone." Willowvine wished she'd kept her bow, but then realized it would have broken when the spell took hold of her. It was going to be a knife fight. She couldn't trust Rainblossom to surrender.

"And you said you wanted to capture me," Rainblossom said as she searched her pockets for a weapon, or perhaps something to stop the bleeding. "No one tells the truth."

"The horses," Willowvine said. "That was on your order, right?"

"Animals, not people," Rainblossom said. She drew her hand out of the pocket and threw stones at Willowvine, stumbling with the effort.

"Is that all you have to protect you?" Willowvine asked. If

Rainblossom wouldn't put up a fight...she couldn't bring herself to kill someone who couldn't defend herself.

"I know magic," Rainblossom said, her voice weak. "I didn't expect a battle. You were supposed to arrive after I found the Stone."

Willowvine took a step forward. Rainblossom stumbled backward toward the Well as if she no longer controlled her muscles. Taking a seed from her pocket, she looked at it, seeming to have forgotten Willowvine, or perhaps she'd dismissed her as a threat.

"Just kneel and I'll tie you up. We can get a healer to—"

"No." Rainblossom's voice cracked, cutting through Willowvine's words. She stared at the seed.

"What spell could that hold to stop me?" Willowvine asked.

"It's not for you," Rainblossom said. She stumbled a few more paces to the edge of the Well.

Willowvine rushed forward to pull her to safety. Dead beast or not, letting her die in the Well Between Worlds felt wrong and dangerous.

Rainblossom held the seed up. "I've lost. I don't want to see our world fall apart." She placed the seed in her mouth and bit down.

Willowvine watched in horror as the look of defeat on Rainblossom's face turned to agony. She folded in half as though a rope around her waist was jerked.

Willowvine lunged and grabbed Rainblossom, pulling her so she landed on the stones rather than plunging into the darkness of the Well.

She rolled Rainblossom over, but there was nothing to be done. The woman was dead, the spell still leaching the heat from her body.

Willowvine knelt beside Rainblossom, gasping for breath. Overcoming the paralysis spell had taken everything from her.

She couldn't rest. Rainblossom might not be the only

person coming for the Stone. Willowvine knew she wouldn't be able to lift it herself, but finding the Stone was the first step. Then she could rest until Springheart and the others arrived.

She pushed herself to her feet and scanned the area. She was still alone.

A groan echoed from the Well.

Willowvine spun around to face whatever was coming. Her only weapon the last throwing knife in the sheath.

A pool of blood drained over the edge of the Well. What had they woken?

Chapter 30

Willowvine dropped to the stones and lay still. If evil was coming through, she didn't want to be the first target. Reminding herself the beast was dead didn't help calm her heart. It beat so hard she felt her body was rocking. Something made the noise, but no one or nothing came into sight.

Time passed. The sun rose, and nothing more came from the Well. Willowvine remembered the last time. There had been dust and wind before the beast spoke. Warning signs they hadn't recognized, but warnings even so. Had she missed something this time?

"Willowvine!"

Tom's voice.

She turned to warn them away, but all three of her companions were running across the path toward her. She realized what they were seeing and stood to show she wasn't hurt.

Tom pulled her into a hug, sobbing his relief into the top of her head. When had he gotten so tall? "We came as fast as we could," he said.

Willowvine disengaged from his arms. "I know. I'm not hurt. We need to find the Stone. It's here."

Springheart looked down at Rainblossom.

"It's a long story," she said. "I think we have some time to breathe before the next attack."

Dawnriver, looking even more pale than usual, scanned the stones of the path and stepped toward the Well.

"No." She grabbed his arm and pulled him back. "Something woke."

"Another beast?" Springheart asked.

"I don't know." She told them everything that happened from the time she'd opened her eyes in the Library right up to the fight with Rainblossom.

"How do we find it?" Tom asked. He stomped on a few pavers as though the Orphan Stone would pop out with the right force.

Dawnriver touched Tom's shoulder and shook his head. He pointed at the Well.

"His voice is still gone," Springheart said.

Dawnriver pulled a scrap of paper and a pencil from his pocket and wrote. The paper looked well used, smears of writing that hadn't been erased completely covered the surface.

It's here to contain the beast.

When she read the words, Willowvine's familiar anger flooded her body. This was simply another way of keeping her from being part of the community.

"I know," she said. "But that beast is dead. There is nothing to prove we need powerful artifacts here any longer. We know that the other Stones are drifting without this one. Like they are missing their anchor. We can't make a choice without taking a risk."

"What else came from inside?" Springheart asked.

"Nothing," Willowvine said. "The sound might not have been from something alive."

"You said it was a groan." Tom stepped to the edge of the Well before she could stop him. "That could mean pain."

She reached to pull him back. "Not everything needs healing."

SPRINGHEART JOINED Tom at the edge. A place he'd never thought to revisit. "I think we need to find out what's in there," he said.

"You mean go inside?" Willowvine asked. "We have no ropes, no harness."

"We can get them," Springheart said, "if we need to. But we have enough on us to construct a rope of sorts. Our cloaks will get me lower than the last time."

"No," Willowvine said. "If anyone goes, It's me. I'm the lightest."

"Me," Dawnriver said. His voice was cracked and barely above a whisper. "It should be me."

Willowvine glared at the healer. Springheart couldn't understand her anger, but he knew there was a secret beneath it.

Dawnriver placed a hand on his throat. "Tell them," he said.

"I thought you already did that," Willowvine said. "The attack came at a convenient time for keeping secrets." She drew everyone away from the Well. "He's not a teacher," she said. "He's an agent. One on our side, if you believe things are that simple. He works for Treepond. The rest can wait until we're done and he can talk."

Springheart looked at Tom. The news wasn't a complete surprise; it was clear that Dawnriver had been hiding something from the beginning. Tom turned away from Dawnriver.

"Why should it be you?" Springheart asked.

"Don't make him talk," Tom said, turning back to them. "Dawnriver, do you have any idea how to recognize the Stone?"

Dawnriver shook his head.

"No one goes unless there's no choice," Tom said. "I'm sorry, but I don't want to lose anyone."

Springheart wanted them all safe, too. Dawnriver had a lot to answer for, but he had to be alive to do that. If Tom was willing to give Dawnriver a chance, then they needed to find another way.

WILLOWVINE REMEMBERED something else about the Well. "We need to move away," she said. "If the beast is alive, or another beast is there, we can't be rational. It influences our thinking."

She led them back across the path to the ground surrounding the maze. As soon as she felt earth beneath her feet, her anger fled. That was not a good omen.

"Nothing more has come from there," she said. "Maybe we don't need to go in. Maybe we were being lured inside."

"We need to look," Springheart said. "At the edge. We should be safe to look inside."

Dawnriver pointed at Tom and then the ground.

"Yes," Willowvine said. "Tom, you must stay here. If we need help, you are the best one to go for it."

"Dawnriver can do that," Tom said.

Tiredness swept through her. Any time spent arguing was time for the thing in the Well to gain strength. Before she could muster an answer, Dawnriver stepped in. He pointed at himself, then Willowvine and Springheart. He moved closer to them and pointed at Tom. What was he trying to say?

"I know I'm not an elf," Tom said. "But that means you should stay. Elves run faster than humans."

Dawnriver sighed and pulled out his paper, erasing the words from before. *It may only be a threat to elves.*

"But it took Lady Madeline," Tom said. "She was human."

Willowvine watched Dawnriver erase and write again.

Yes, Madeline was human, and she killed the beast. If we need to fight another beast, we might need you to do that.

"Dawnriver is right," Willowvine said. "It has only been harmful to elves. Please stand here and be our protector."

"I can't see what happens from here," Tom said. "It's too far."

"I'm afraid its influence permeated the stones," Springheart said. "If we need help, we'll make sure you know."

Tom muttered something, then agreed. He stalked over to the pile of bags they'd dropped on arriving. "We should get started with that rope."

WILLOWVINE LAY ON HER STOMACH, head just over the opening. "It looks the same," she said. "I thought something would have changed when the beast died."

"It's only the house," Springheart said. "But I agree, it seems wrong that there is no evidence of the battle here."

She couldn't hear anything from inside the Well. If the beast had survived, it was cannier now.

Dawnriver ran his hand over the stones at the rim. Then, shaking his head, he tried to reach farther down.

"Don't," Willowvine said. "It's easy to fall in."

He turned and sat up, facing away from the Well. He raised his arm and waved. She saw Tom run toward them.

"What?"

Dawnriver put his hand on his throat. "Light."

Tom came close enough to hear the request then ran back to their packs. Lanterns were a good idea.

"Does it hurt to talk?" she asked.

"The healers said he should not speak. They think he can avoid permanent damage if he rests his voice for a few days," Springheart said.

"No pain," Dawnriver said.

Tom returned with the lanterns already lit. "Can I look?" he asked. "Just a quick peek."

She shook her head. "It's too dangerous."

He pointed at his waist, two cloaks were twisted and wrapped around him. "Rope. You can hold it so I don't fall in." His face was so hopeful.

She understood the draw. It wasn't a compulsion from any evil inside the Well, only curiosity. To come this far, to such an important site, and be restricted to standing on the sidelines; she wouldn't have obeyed it either.

"You don't try to go in," she said. "One peek and you're done."

He grinned. "I promise."

The rope was already secured around his waist. Spring-heart and Dawnriver took hold of each end and stepped back until there was some tension, then they leaned away.

Willowvine placed one lantern on the edge of the Well and handed the other to Tom. "No matter what happens, we'll pull you back," she said.

He stepped to the edge, Springheart and Dawnriver matching his pace to keep the rope taut. Her heart thudded as he leaned forward. Knowing his need to see it didn't make the Well less dangerous.

"What does this Stone look like?" Tom asked.

"We don't know, but probably something like the others," Willowvine said.

"It's here," Tom said. "Just on the second layer."

He leaned forward more. Willowvine turned and yelled, "Pull him back."

Tom jerked backwards onto his butt.

A howl of wind rushed from the Well, and the lanterns blew out.

Chapter 31

"The Stone is inside?" Willowvine asked as soon as they left the path. "How do you know?"

"It looks different from the others," Tom said. "I noticed right away. Why didn't you see it?"

"We hadn't looked that closely," Springheart said. "And the last time we were here, we were in search of something else."

Dawnriver was checking Tom for injuries. He finished his examination and then turned back to her. "We need to go now," he said, hand on throat.

"I'm going in," Springheart said. "You hold the ropes, and I'll see if I can withdraw the Stone."

"You can't just pull it out," Dawnriver said.

Is he trying to ruin his voice?

"Stop talking," she said. "We have to get a closer look. I think we'll need tools, but we won't know until someone goes in."

"I *am* going in," Springheart said. "I'm not arguing. Tie your cloaks together and be happy it's so close to the top."

He stalked away without waiting for her to agree. She did think he was the best one to go even though her heart ached with worry. Dawnriver was too injured, Tom wasn't an elf, and she probably wouldn't have the strength to lift the Stone alone no matter how loose.

She told Tom and Dawnriver to make the rope and ran after Springheart.

"It won't take them long," she said as she joined him at the edge. "I told them to cut the cloaks into strips and braid them together, so the rope would be stronger."

He nodded but kept his gaze on the hole. "Did you notice that it's warm and sunny here, all except for the Well? That's not a normal shadow; it's like the dark is a living thing inside."

It did feel like they were looking at something more than a hole. "But we can go in, so it's still part of our world."

"Let's hope so."

"Why can't we see the Stone?" she asked. "Tom said it was obvious."

"Maybe the same reason Madeline succeeded in killing the beast," Springheart said. "He's not an elf."

Dawnriver joined them with the braided rope. He helped Springheart tie a loop around his waist, leaving two long ends.

Willowvine took one end and walked backwards until she felt his weight pull at her. "Be careful," she said. "I don't want to explain to Leafcreek why you got killed."

Springheart smiled at her and then turned and lowered himself into the dark.

She wanted to be there watching but knew that would leave Springheart vulnerable. Here, holding onto his means of escape with Dawnriver, was the right thing. "What can you see?" she called out.

He replied. She could hear that he'd said something, but the sound didn't carry enough for her to make out the words.

The tension on the rope relaxed slightly. He must have found a way to brace himself. Had he found the right Stone?

The rope jerked, almost pulling her off her feet. She

braced and looked to Dawnriver. He was steadier and trying to say something.

"Pull him out," she said.

They heaved on the ropes and Springheart's head rose above the ground. He pulled his body onto the stones surrounding the hole and lay flat. As soon as he reached the safety of the ground, she dropped the rope and ran to him.

"You're hurt." She saw the blood on his hands. Dawnriver reached out to Springheart and she slapped his hands away.

"Get Tom," she said. "Save your energy to heal yourself."

"It's just a scrape," Springheart said, but he let Dawnriver go.

"Did you find it?" She dabbed at his wound with her sleeve.

"Yes. Something has changed and it's like Tom said. There are probably more stones of power used in the Well. It's no longer a smooth surface with identical stones. They are all different. I was able to get a toehold on one. I pulled at the Orphan Stone and it moved a little. Then my hand slipped and so did I."

She looked up to see the healers hurrying towards them. "We can't take the time to go back to the Library for tools. We have to figure out a way to free the Stone now."

As she finished speaking, a moan rose from the Well. She covered her ears as the moan turned into a scream that went on forever.

THEY STOOD BACK on safe ground, the Well quiet for now. Willowvine paced back and forth as they debated how to remove the Stone. Everyone was willing to volunteer, but no one had come up with an idea that had a chance of success.

"Maybe Tom should go to the Library for help," Springheart said. "It's been silent for a while, perhaps the beast is not fully awake yet."

Willowvine wasn't so optimistic, as only a half hour had passed. After healing Springheart, Tom had started emptying their packs hoping to find something that would help.

"I can't go fast enough," he said. "It should be Dawnriver."

Willowvine looked to Dawnriver but he shook his head. "I won't be able to convince them." The words were now only a little more than a wheeze.

"Save your voice." She looked over the stone path. They had no option to walk away. This wasn't just about the orphans. The other Stones were moving, and she knew in her bones the only way to stop that was to restore all three. "We can scry the Library," she said. "We don't need to go there."

"There's no water nearby for the spell," Springheart said. "Do you have a scrying crystal? Or some other way to reach out?"

"I hoped Dawnriver would use his," she said. "You reached out to Treepond. Can you get the Library?"

He pulled out the crystal, making motions that seemed to say he was the only one who could activate the spell. He mouthed Treepond's name, not to activate it, but clearly to say the crystal was anchored to her.

"She can contact the Library," Willowvine said. "Tell her what's going on."

He held the crystal close to his lips and spoke her name. It was no more than a breath of sound. The crystal stayed clear.

"Then we're on our own," she said.

"Are these precious?" Tom asked. He was holding her throwing knives.

"Where did you find them?" She'd used them in the fight with Rainblossom, whose body was still on the stones. They'd only taken the time to drag her out of the way, not bury her.

"One on the grass," he said. "I took the other from Rain-blossom."

"They're just knives," she said in answer to his earlier question.

"No, they're not." He smiled. "Use them as tools to pull the Stone out. Work at the mortar, wiggle the Stone out a bit. We'll need something to hold it so we don't lose it to another world."

"Bring one of the travel packs," Willowvine said. "They won't break under the weight."

Moments later they were standing looking down into the Well. For the first time in days, Willowvine wasn't worrying over the future. "I'll go," she said. "I think it's right that an orphan does this, and Springheart's blood is already inside."

She felt the rope go around her waist. She hung the pack straps over her arm and slid the two knives into their sheaths.

"There are plenty of places to balance on," Springheart whispered. "Just don't take too long because I don't think they are stable."

She nodded, knelt on the edge, then turned and let her legs drop into the hole. She felt around for a foothold and found one, then she climbed down. What had once been a smooth surface was now a series of ill-fitting rocks that no elf would have agreed to build. Whatever spells they'd used on this struc-ture were crumbling. Stone dust rose from the depths, making it hard for her to breathe.

She reached the Orphan Stone after only a few steps. It sat balanced on the brick below, a brick that had once looked like a smooth stone. She tried to pull the Orphan Stone toward the sack, but it was jammed in at the back.

Willowvine slid her blade along the side and wiggled. The Stone moved, and she continued to work until she could tip it into the sack. The weight of the Stone pulled her off her perch and she dangled for a moment until they yanked her up to lie on the pavers in the sun.

She heaved the bag up and got to her knees. "We did it."

The ground started to shake, the pavers rocking and shifting. Willowvine felt herself slide back to the hole. She gripped the pack and crawled forward. The others stumbled backward, holding the rope, helping to keep her from falling.

She stood and stumbled toward them, the weight of the Orphan Stone stopping her from gaining speed.

When they were far enough from the edge, Willowvine let Springheart help her carry her burden. They scrambled to the grassy clearing and collapsed onto the pile of clothing and bags.

Willowvine let the Stone rest on the ground and stared across the once smooth path. Every stone was out of position. Some glowed with power, others were mundane rocks. Rainblossom's body slid down the side of a large slab of granite that rose like a sentinel from the surrounding chaos. All Willowvine could feel was a slight vibration in the soil around her.

Within minutes, the pristine construction of the maze and Well became a field of rubble.

Chapter 32

Their return to the island had been a blur for Willowvine. She remembered stopping at the Library and explaining what happened before rushing out on fresh horses. Dawnriver had stayed to help the librarians claim all the valued artifacts from the debris.

Then it was a simple matter of riding back to the City and boarding the ship. They hadn't slept for two full days. They just changed horses every few hours at the little villages along the way. Tom was exhausted from feeding them all with enough energy to keep going. On board, all three had fallen asleep as soon as they closed the curtain to their cabin. Willowvine slept curled protectively around the Stone.

Now she stood beside Grasshorn, waiting for her turn to start the rite that would put the Stone in place. Lakewing led them, Springheart behind, Grasshorn, and then Willowvine last with the Orphan Stone. Leafcreek watched from a bench, Tom beside him.

She tried to clear her mind, but the others distracted her. The council had sent representatives, Treepond one of the three. They stood behind the bench, watching. Only Treepond smiling.

Then she took her first step and everything that was not the path in front of her fled. It seemed only moments later, Willowvine placed the Orphan Stone in the gap between the others. Grasshorn and Lakewing as the new Guardians said the last words of the rite.

The Stones moved, slowly enough that at first, she thought it was in her imagination. They were coming together. When they settled, Willowvine saw how they fit to make the symbol for strength. Before she could comment, they sank below the surface.

"What?" She turned to the Guardians. "Did we do something wrong?"

Lakewing shook her head. "Cartref is protecting them. They are still there, but eventually, only the Guardians will know."

When Leafcreek asked to delay the celebratory meal until he'd rested, Willowvine couldn't stay inside. The presence of the council leaders made the small house oppressive. She couldn't find Tom or Springheart, so she took her coat and went for another walk. It was probably the last day she would spend on the island, so it was good to enjoy as much of it as she could.

TREEPOND MET her at the door when she was tired enough to return. "I'm sorry, Willowvine. Leafcreek did not wake from his sleep. He has left this world."

She'd only been gone a short time. How had he died so quickly? Yes, he'd been frail at the ceremony, but... "He saw the rites," she said, wiping tears from her cheeks. "He held on for that."

"Yes, he died happy that his vision was achieved. The new

Guardians are preparing his body. We should wait in the kitchen. There's food."

She didn't want to eat, but there was nothing else she could do. They would lay Leafcreek to rest at sundown. "He liked to sit and watch the sea," she said.

"They know," Treepond said. "We'll gather at his favorite spot later."

In the kitchen, Willowvine joined Springheart and Tom near the back door. The council members sat at the table. Everyone held a mug of tea, but no one drank.

Treepond sat with her fellow councilors. "While we wait to pay honor to our friend," she said, "it is a good time to tell you our position."

Can't they wait to betray me until Leafcreek is at rest?

Springheart put his hand on her arm. "Just listen."

She felt Tom beside her stiffen, ready to come to her aid if the council turned her good work into a punishment again.

"We have signed the order to make all orphans part of society. All have amnesty for any crimes they committed to survive."

Willowvine expected to feel something more than just acceptance. "Thank you. I will find a way to spread the news."

Treepond smiled. "You could tell us where your friends are. There's no reason to keep that secret now."

"It's their secret, not mine," she said. "You know the importance of that."

"Very well. One more thing. Perhaps a word of caution is in order. We have changed the laws and we will send out messengers to apprise everyone, but we cannot control the hearts of our people. There will be some who never accept you into their world."

Willowvine remembered the beginning of the journey. The young pregnant elf named Elderroot. "There are many who will," she said.

"I would also like to offer a position to you," Treepond said. "No more wandering the world facing dangers."

Springheart removed his hand. Willowvine looked at him and saw loss in his eyes; she felt the ache of Leafcreek's death, too.

"You should tell them what you want," he said.

"Thank you for the offer," she said. "I'm glad that my fellow orphans will have a chance at a better life, but I'm happy to continue to wander the world."

Treepond looked disappointed and Willowvine didn't want to discuss it any longer. She excused herself and stepped through the back door to sit on the bench.

"I thought you would accept," Springheart said. "I thought that you wanted to be part of the Elven world."

She patted the bench beside her. "I realized I only wanted the option," she said. "But if you want to start a new life, I'll understand."

"And who would stop you from running headlong into problems?" he asked.

Tom slipped through the door to join them. "Can we make our first adventure a visit to collect Dawnriver?"

"Do you think he has his voice back?" Willowvine asked, joking.

"I hope so," Tom said. "He still owes me some training."

Want More?

If you enjoyed reading The Elven Stones: Orphan please consider helping other readers to find the story by leaving a review.

Looking for more great fantasy reads from P A Wilson. Use the QR code to see what's new on her site.

Free ebook

Claim your copy of Obstacles of Magic when you use the QR code to sign up for my newsletter and learn more about Madeline's history with magic.

Also by P A Wilson

For more books by P A Wilson

Use the QR code below or go to pawilson.ca

About the Author

Perry Wilson is a Canadian author based in Vancouver, BC who has big ideas and an itch to tell stories. Having spent some time on university, a career, and life in general, she returned to writing in 2008 and hasn't looked back since (well, maybe a little, but only while parallel parking).

She is a member of the Vancouver Writers Social Group, The Royal City Literary Arts Society, and The Surrey Writing Workshop. Perry has self-published several novels. She writes the Madeline Journeys, a fantasy series about a high-powered lawyer who finds herself trapped in a magical world, the Quinn Larson Quests, which follows the adventures of a wizard named Quinn who must contend with volatile fae in the heart of Vancouver, and the Charity Deacon Investigations, a mystery thriller series about a private eye who tends to fall into serious trouble with her cases, and The Riverton Romances, a series based in a small town in Oregon, one of her favorite states. Her stand-alone novels are Breaking the Bonds, Closing the Circle, and The Dragon at The Edge of The Map.

For more information
www.pawilson.ca
pawilson@pawilson.ca

Acknowledgments

People think that the process of writing is solitary. That's not the case for me. I have help from so many people it would be hard to acknowledge everyone, but I'll give it a try.

The support and inspiration I get from my writer's groups is incalculable. The Vancouver Writers Social Group opens my mind to other ways of telling a story. The Royal City Literary Arts Society gives me the opportunity to meet and share with other writers who have more knowledge than I do. The Other 11 Months group is where I learn about getting the words on the page. And my critique group who helps me find the best parts of the story I want to tell. Thanks to all of the members of these great groups.

Last of all, but definitely a huge part of the process, my beta readers. These are the people who love stories and are willing, and more than able, to tell me if my finished story is ready for you, my readers.